BOSS GAMES

BOSS #7

VICTORIA QUINN

CONTENTS

Hartwick Publishing

Boss Games

Copyright © 2018 by Victoria Quinn

1

DIESEL

I REMEMBERED the day my mother died—vividly.

It was the worst day of my life.

I was in college at the time. I had just finished my last final and was on my way to my apartment when I got the phone call.

My dad told me the news.

He barely said anything over the phone, his silence packed with so much sorrow that I could feel it over the line. I remembered how cold I felt, how empty life felt. I'd always been close to my mother, and I took for granted how wonderful she was. I just assumed she would always be there.

Until the day she wasn't.

Now I was reliving that nightmare, but this day was far worse.

It was worse because Titan was the love of my life.

The only woman I'd ever loved.

We hadn't had enough time together. It was far too soon. I was supposed to go first, due to old age. I wasn't supposed to live without her. She was the stronger one; she should be the one to live without me.

I couldn't do this.

My driver took Thorn and me to the hospital, but we didn't say a word to each other in the back seat. The corners were still covered with snow, patches of it sitting in the gutters. People walked in thick jackets down the sidewalk. Life in the city continued on peacefully, while chaos reigned in my heart.

Thorn stared out the window, his hands still shaking.

Mine were shaking too.

The car wasn't moving fast enough. Time was moving too slowly. Titan was in critical condition, a bullet in her chest. She lost a lot of blood, and there'd been no update about her condition since she was rushed to the hospital.

I felt like I had a bullet in my chest too.

A lifetime later, the driver pulled up to the hospital.

Thorn and I maneuvered inside, got to the ICU, and checked in with the nurse at the front desk. When I looked at the nurse in her green scrubs, I nearly forgot how to talk like a human being. I couldn't think correctly, so I just said what I could. "Tatum Titan...I'm her fiancé."

The nurse obviously recognized me, judging by her look of pity. She turned to her computer, typed in Titan's name, and pulled up her chart.

Thorn stood back, his breathing still haywire. He hadn't calmed down since he'd read the headlines on his phones. He repeatedly dragged his hand down his face or through his hair. He was taking the news just as hard as I was—and just as silently.

"She's..." I'd never struggled with words. I took control of every situation, spitting out my thoughts the second they came into my mind. But now, my eloquence was gone. I'd been stripped down to a grieving man...and I could barely function. "She's alive, right?"

"Mr. Hunt, I don't have any details on her status." Her eyes were on her screen. "It says she was rushed to surgery the second she arrived. The bullet hit a major artery in her chest. The surgeons are working to stop the bleeding and safely remove the bullet.

That's all I know." She turned back to me, her face showing she felt even worse for me.

I gripped the counter, taking in those words like each one was a single bullet. "Is she going to be okay?" It was a stupid question because I knew I wouldn't get an answer. But I needed to know she would make it through this. She was my whole life. Without her, I was nothing. None of my accomplishments amounted to the importance of earning her love.

"I can't say, Mr. Hunt. The second I get an update, I'll let you know."

I stayed rooted to the spot, gripping the counter for balance.

My father must have arrived with my brothers because he appeared at my side. His large hand moved to my back, and he gently pulled me away from the counter. "Let's take a seat, Diesel. They'll update us as soon as they know anything."

I didn't say anything, but I let him guide me to one of the couches in the waiting room. There were other families there, sitting in their corners and watching the TVs on the walls. The sound was off, and it showed the local news. Right now, all they could talk about was the shooting that had just happened. They played footage from the cameras in the lobby.

I didn't look.

My body sank into the cushion, and I gripped the wooden armrest.

My father sat beside me.

Thorn sat on my other side.

And we just waited there.

I stared at my hands in my lap, my back hunched over. Just last night, she lay underneath me and asked me to marry her. She didn't want to wait. She didn't give a damn what anyone thought of our love affair. She wanted me forever and always. I gave her my ring, and I pledged my eternal love for her.

It was the greatest night of my life.

Now I sat in the waiting room at the hospital, hoping for good news.

Everything had changed in an instant.

My happiness was gone.

Gone.

I still didn't know all the details of the shooting. All I gathered was Bruce rushed Titan when she got off the elevator. He gunned her down in the lobby of her building. I didn't know what happened to him. The second I knew Titan had been shot, that was all I cared about.

If I'd just waited for her, I could have protected her.

I could be the one in surgery right now.

And she would be sitting in my place instead.

Why the fuck didn't I just wait?

My biggest regret.

My father pressed his hand to the center of my back. He didn't tell me everything would be alright or try to distract me from my thoughts, but he reminded me he was there, along with everyone else in the room.

Thorn turned his gaze to the TV and watched the footage.

I still couldn't look.

I couldn't watch my baby get shot.

My baby... I'd do anything to call her that again.

Thorn released a deep breath before he turned forward again, his jaw clenched. "She killed him. That's my girl..."

I still didn't look. "She did?"

"Yeah," Thorn answered. "She got his gun from him and shot him in the face and neck."

That was the only good news I'd gotten so far. "Good."

"He was going to shoot her again, but she stopped him," Thorn continued. "She's a fighter...

and I know she's fighting right now." His voice broke at the end so he stopped speaking.

"She is a fighter," I whispered. Titan would do anything she could to get back to me. She was young, healthy, and strong. If anyone could overcome this, it was her. She'd been shot once, but she managed to get the gun from Bruce and destroy him. There was still hope. There was still hope I would get my baby back.

God, please.

I leaned forward and pressed my face into my hands, shutting out the room altogether. I wanted time to pass quickly, to hear the doctor say the surgery was a success. I wanted to know we still had our lives together, that I still had something to live for.

My father rubbed his hand down my back. "She'll win, son. She always does."

I nodded. "I know, Dad."

2

TITAN

UNAWARE of where I was or if I was anyone at all...I felt like nothing but a spirit. There was no light, no sensation. There was just a small sense of existence, not really on earth, but somewhere in space.

I was certain I was dead.

I thought I heard the loud beep of the monitor.

I thought I felt Diesel's spirit collapse.

I thought I experienced things I couldn't understand.

And then I saw something.

In an old building in Brooklyn, I stood inside the small studio apartment my father and I used to occupy. The paint was coming off the walls, the floorboards were crooked, the refrigerator constantly hummed like it was on its last leg, and the yellow couch still had the endless holes where the stuffing was seeping through.

It was home.

I used to sleep on one of the couches, while my father used the pullout bed. We had an old kitchen table we'd found at the flea market. It had two plastic cups on top, dishes that I forgot to wash. There was one picture of us on the counter, a day of us at the park.

It smelled the same as it used to.

I felt my expensive stilettos click against the hard floor as I moved. I was in my Suede clothing, an outfit Connor had specifically made just for me. I was the same age that I was before the bullet entered my chest.

But I never forgot how I used to be.

The sunlight filtered through the dusty windows, showing a view of the meat-packing facility across the street.

"Look at you."

I stopped when I heard his voice, the deep sound that still found me in my dreams. It was full of a constant smile, full of my childhood memories. I stopped breathing when I heard it, a waterfall of emotions cascading over me. He'd been gone for ten years, but he never left my heart.

I slowly turned around and looked at my father. He wore the only pair of glasses he'd ever owned, square frames with thick lenses. His brown hair was turning gray, and it was shaggy and untamed. He wore his light-colored jeans and his blue t-shirt, one of the outfits he wore the most. His fingers were callused from the constant grip of the paintbrush.

He was exactly the same. "Daddy…"

He closed the gap between us and gripped me by the elbows, the smell of his cologne washing over me. "Tatum, you've grown into a beautiful woman. You look just like your mother… I can hardly believe it."

He never mentioned my mother when he was alive. "I think I look like you too."

His smile softened gently. "Definitely." He ran his hands up my arms before he stepped back. "Richest woman in the world… I want to say I'm surprised, but I'm not. I always knew you would do great things. But such immense things…I couldn't have anticipated."

My eyes filled with tears, but not tears of pain. They were tears from something else entirely. "I wanted to take care of you. I wanted to give you a better life… I'm sorry I couldn't do it fast enough."

"A better life?" He tilted his head to the side,

shooting me that surprised look he used to give me when I said something that didn't make sense. "Tatum, I had a great life. I wish I could have given you better school clothes and paid for you to go to college...but I had everything else I needed. I had you. That's always been more than enough."

"Daddy..." Now the tears fell down my cheeks, two streams on my face.

"Sweetheart." He gripped my elbows again. "Don't be sad. You have no idea how proud I am of you."

"I know you are... I've always known."

"And you published my book." His lenses magnified the moisture in his eyes, showing the hint of tears. "You made my dream come true."

"Of course I did."

"That was very sweet of you." He slowly rubbed his hands up and down my arms. "You have no idea how nice it is to see you again. But, I've been dreading this day too. It shouldn't have come so soon."

His words sank into me, their meaning heavy. "That means..."

"Yes."

"Oh..."

He squeezed my arms gently. "Unless there's something worth fighting for. Is there, Tatum?"

Diesel's face came into my mind. I suddenly felt his ring on my finger, felt the weight of the small diamond. I raised my hand and showed it to my father.

He examined it with his same boyish smile. "It's beautiful."

"Thank you...you would love him."

"I already do. Diesel Hunt...he's a fine young man."

I looked into his face again, feeling the swelling of my eyes and cheeks.

"Then it looks like there is something worth fighting for..."

I nodded. "Yes, there is. I want to stay with you... I miss you. But—"

"Go, sweetheart. Like I said, it's too soon for you." He released me and stepped back. "You have so many more things you need to do, Tatum. You've become the richest woman in the world at the age of thirty. What else are you capable of?"

"I've always wanted a family of my own."

"Good. There's no greater joy than having a child. I know from experience."

My smile melted away as the tears kept coming.

He grabbed both of my hands and brought them together. "Go, sweetheart. Fight your way back to him. We'll have our time later."

"We didn't have enough time in the first place…"

"We have eternity." He squeezed my hands before he let go. "Can you give a message to Diesel?"

"Yes."

"Tell him he has my blessing."

A smile returned to my lips.

"And tell him to forgive himself."

Just as quickly, my smile faded away. "Forgive himself for what?"

"For not taking that bullet for you."

3

DIESEL

TWELVE HOURS HAD PASSED.

No news.

I checked in with the nurse at the front desk, but she had nothing new to report. She ended her shift and was replaced by someone else. Then I started bugging her just as I bugged the previous woman.

My dad stayed by my side the whole time.

Thorn didn't sleep, seeming as troubled as he had been when he'd first heard the news.

I hadn't shut my eyes even for a second, unable to relax until I heard something. I didn't drink or eat, and when a headache started, I didn't care.

Thorn's parents arrived an hour ago. We made our introductions, but I couldn't remember their names because I hadn't been listening. Brett talked to me about sports for a little bit, obviously trying to get my mind off the current situation.

Nothing could get my mind off it.

I wished Bruce Carol wasn't dead just so I could kill him again.

But a bullet to the brain would be too good for him.

He needed to suffer.

At my bare hands.

Fifteen hours later, a doctor in blue scrubs finally stepped into the waiting room. With gray hair and glasses, he scanned the room in search of someone.

I hoped he was looking for me.

I stood up and stared at him, wanting to make sure he didn't miss me. Other people were waiting for news about their loved ones, so I wasn't the only one anxious for an update.

But I must have been the one he was looking for because he walked up to me.

Fuck.

Please, God.

My father and brothers gathered around me, along with Thorn and his parents.

I stood with my hands on my hips, my breathing already escalating even though I hadn't received the news. If she didn't make it, then I didn't want to hear him say anything. I couldn't handle those horrifying words.

I'd already heard them once. I couldn't listen to them again.

"Ms. Titan's family?" the doctor asked.

Not a single one of us was related to her. She didn't have a living relative. The family she did have had come from something thicker than blood. I loved her more than anyone she'd ever known, and that was good enough. "Yes."

He placed his hands on his hips. "She had a lot of internal damage from the bullet. It pierced her chest, hit a large artery, nicked some of her heart, and did a lot of damage to her soft tissues. She lost half of her blood volume, and she needed an emergency transfusion..." He continued to name off all her injuries.

I could barely take it.

"Toward the end of the surgery, we lost her for a bit..."

I immediately staggered even though I'd been standing upright before that.

As if my father had expected that to happen, he caught me in both of his arms. He stabilized me on the floor, keeping my feet planted in place.

"What does that mean?" I demanded.

"She flatlined," the doctor continued. "We did a few rounds of CPR and brought her back. She stabilized after that, and we completed the operation successfully. I want to keep a critical eye on her for the next twenty-four hours just in case. So she'll stay in the ICU for now. Afterward, she'll move to the surgical floor."

He began with such horrifying news that I nearly missed the good news. "So she's alright?"

"For now, yes," he said. "Considering how much damage she sustained, she did surprisingly well. She's strong and healthy, that's for sure. She'll be asleep for the next few hours, and I want to monitor her for signs of infection. She'll be here for at least a week."

I didn't give a shit how long she was there. I just cared that she was okay.

That she would live. "Thank you..." I didn't know his name. He'd probably told me, but I hadn't been listening. "I need to see her. When can I see her?"

"We can only have two visitors at a time," the doctor said. "Due to her risk of infection. You'll need to scrub down and change your clothing."

"That's fine." I just wanted to see her.

"I'll take you to her," he said. "Who's coming?"

That didn't take long to figure out. "Come on, Thorn."

He walked with me, knowing we were the two people in the world she would want to see the most.

TUBES WERE EVERYWHERE, A MACHINE WAS BREATHING for her, and she looked paler than I'd ever seen her. This strong and unbreakable woman had been desecrated by that madman. He tried to take her life, but he only took her strength—for a short time.

It was hard to look at her.

I should have protected her.

I stayed at her bedside in the hospital gown they gave me. Gloves were on my hands, and Thorn was dressed in the same ensemble.

Thorn and I still didn't talk. We both stared at Titan.

"I owe you an apology."

I turned to Thorn, unsure if I'd heard him speak because he hadn't said anything in so long.

"I should have believed you," he continued, his eyes on Titan. "If we'd both believed you from the beginning, this may never have happened."

"You don't owe me an apology, Thorn." The only

person who should be apologizing was me. It was my job to protect Titan, but I didn't. I failed her.

I fucking failed her.

"I'm sorry anyway," he whispered.

I watched her breathe into the tube, her chest rising and falling. She looked so small in the bed. She wasn't in her stilettos and her designer clothes. She didn't have her usual elegance and poise. She was a woman fighting to stay alive.

As if Thorn could feel my pain, he comforted me. "She's going to be alright. The hardest part is over."

"You think?" I stared at her small hand as it rested beside her.

"I do."

I stared at my hands, feeling my breath come out shaky. "I keep telling myself that...because I couldn't bear it if..." I refused to finish the sentence, to say the horrific words out loud. It was a fate I couldn't contemplate. I'd rather die than live in a world where she didn't exist.

"She's the strongest person I've ever known. She'll make it."

I nodded in agreement. "She is a badass."

"Yes, she is. She'd been shot in the chest, but she still kicked his ass. She'll pull through."

"You're right." It was the first time I felt slightly better. But until her eyes opened and she gripped my hand, I would still be uneasy.

I would be uneasy until I could tell her I loved her—and she could say it back.

———

THORN DRIFTED OFF TO SLEEP IN THE CHAIR, UNABLE to keep his eyes open after being awake for thirty-six hours.

I hardly closed my eyes unless it was to blink.

Maybe I was delirious with exhaustion, or maybe I was energized by hope. Whatever the reason, my eyes hadn't left her face as I kept waiting—kept hoping.

Finally, her feet moved. Her hand gripped the sheets. She took a deeper breath than usual.

"Tatum." My hand moved to hers on the bed. The latex glove separated my skin from hers, but it was better than nothing. "Baby, I'm here." I didn't need to tell her it was me. She would always recognize my voice.

Her eyes opened, and she looked at me.

She couldn't speak because of the tube in her mouth, but her eyes said everything she couldn't.

She squeezed my hand back, tears welled in her eyes, and she reached for me with her other hand.

I hit the button for the nurse and grabbed her other hand as I stood at the bedside.

The nurse came in a moment later, and they worked with the doctor to remove the tube down her throat. The machine was turned off now that she was breathing on her own. They examined her before they left the room again, giving us some privacy.

She cleared her throat several times, unable to speak right now.

I sat at the edge of the bed and grabbed both of her hands. I wanted to touch more of her, but out of fear for her injuries, I didn't get too close to her. "How are you feeling?"

"I...I don't know." Her thumbs gently grazed over my knuckles. "I guess I feel good."

My natural instinct was to squeeze her hands in relief, to feel her pulse strong against my skin. But I refrained from doing all the things I wanted to do. I wanted to crawl into that bed beside her and wrap my arms around her. "The doctor said you're doing well. They just want to keep you for a while and make sure things continue to improve."

Her eyes were heavy-lidded with fatigue, and she

looked weak despite all the sleeping she'd done. "Diesel...I died."

My hands went cold, my features frozen. The doctor had never mentioned to her that she'd flat-lined during the surgery. "No, you're here. You're here with me, Tatum." I squeezed her hands gently.

"No...I slipped away. I don't know how long it lasted, but I was gone."

I still hadn't taken a breath, too tense to do anything.

"And I saw my father."

She was on a lot of medication, including the aftereffects of anesthesia. So I didn't contradict her or doubt what she'd seen.

"He told me he was proud of me...that he loved me."

I held her gaze, my fingers caressing her.

"I know that's crazy. I know how I must sound... but it happened. When he grabbed me, I felt him. I felt his spirit, and I think he felt mine. He told me I could fight and come back to this side...if I had something to live for. He told me that you have his blessing...and that you should forgive yourself."

"Forgive myself?" I whispered.

"He said you felt guilty for not protecting me..."

I did feel guilty—and that sent shivers down my

spine. It was something I'd been thinking about in the waiting room, had been thinking about since the moment she'd been shot. "I'm sorry I wasn't there for you, baby."

"Don't apologize, Diesel."

"I should have waited for you."

"No, don't do that…"

I took a deep breath and closed my eyes, stilling the emotion that had built up in my chest. I felt the tears before they started, felt the anguish before it truly emerged. Now that she was okay, I could finally let the dam open. I couldn't keep the pain bottled up inside anymore. The tears formed in my eyes.

Two drops dripped down my cheeks.

"Diesel…" She squeezed my hands with her limited strength.

I took a deep breath and stopped the emotion in its tracks, swallowing it so it wouldn't come back. That was the only vulnerability I was going to show. I never showed weakness in front of anyone. She was the one who'd almost died. Everything should be about her, not me. "I should have protected you, Tatum. I should have been standing beside you. I should have taken that bullet. This shouldn't have happened."

"But it did happen, Diesel. And I'm okay. That's all that matters."

She could say whatever she wanted to make me feel better, but it wouldn't change my perspective. I asked her to be my wife, and that meant she was the single most important thing in my life. I'd have to do better from now, to commit myself to her well-being every single day. "It won't happen again." I brought her hands to my lips and kissed them. "I promise."

She squeezed my hands. "I know."

I sat beside her and held her hands in silence. I savored the feel of her pulse against my fingertips, the sign of life underneath her skin. She was still with me. She was still right beside me. And she would still spend her life with me.

"Is he dead?" she whispered.

I nodded. "You killed him."

"Good."

I was glad she didn't feel any remorse for it. Even if she took a life, it was in self-defense. It was her or him—and she'd made the right decision. "You never have to worry about him again."

"I'm sorry I didn't believe you in the first place, Diesel. Now I know I was wrong...and I paid the price."

"Please forget about it." We'd lost some time

together, but we found each other again anyway. It didn't matter what had happened in the past. Only the future mattered, and that future included both of us.

"I'm still sorry, Diesel. I know how much I hurt you."

"And you made up for it by asking me to marry you."

She smiled. "I thought you asked me."

"I did. We both did." My large hands covered most of hers. I was twice her size, overshadowing her in every way. I knew that made her feel safe, and as long as I sat there, she would never have to worry about anything again.

Thorn stirred from his chair in the corner, and after wiping the sleep from his eyes, he looked at Titan. The last thought he had disappeared because Titan was the only thing in his mind. He left the chair and walked to the other side of the bed, his eyes trained exclusively on her. Love and fear were heavy in his eyes. The corporate executive who never showed a single expression was reduced to an emotional man. He stopped beside her and stared down at her, seeing the paleness I noticed the second I looked at her. His eyes roamed over her body, seeing the gauze poke out from underneath her gown. His hands rested at the edge of the bed. "I was so fucking scared, Titan." He released a deep breath, as if he'd been holding it since the moment she'd been shot.

I released one of her hands, knowing I couldn't hog both.

She grabbed his hand and held it tightly. "I'm okay, Thorn."

He pulled up a chair and sat directly beside her, his hand still in hers. "I wouldn't know what to do without you...you're my best friend. You're the only person who really knows me..." When his voice shook, he stopped speaking. He hid the emotion as quickly as it came, forcing his expression to return to masculine stoicism. Maybe it was because I was sitting there. Or maybe he just didn't wear his heart on his sleeve.

I'd have offered to leave, but I refused to walk away from her.

"You're my best friend too," she said quietly. "And I'm not going anywhere. I'm right here, Thorn. I'll be here every day to tell you when you're being an ass and set you straight..."

He cracked a smile.

"This is just a bump in the road. I'll recover and be back to normal soon."

"I know you will." His fingers interlocked with hers. "I'm so proud of you. That asshole had a gun pointed at your face, and you didn't even flinch."

"Like I'd give him the satisfaction." Her voice was still gentle but full of hatred.

"You didn't give up," he continued. "You'd been shot in the chest, but that didn't stop you. There are no words to describe that kind of strength...that kind of bravery."

"It wasn't either one." She squeezed both of our hands. "I just had so much to live for."

ONCE THE STAFF NO LONGER DEEMED HER CRITICAL, they moved her to a new floor. She had a private room with her own living room and kitchen, and her hospital room looked fit enough to be a hotel suite. She was allowed to have more visitors, but I kept everyone away for the next day or two.

I wanted her to rest.

I was starting to get delirious from not sleeping. I hardly ate anything either. I knew she would be alright at that point, but I couldn't leave her. My clothes started to feel uncomfortable, and my hair started to build up too much oil.

But I wasn't leaving.

"Diesel."

I was sitting on the couch near her bed, watching the mute TV while she slept. I turned my gaze to her. "Yes, baby?"

"Go home and get some sleep." She looked small in the large bed, wires still hooked up to her body. Her hands rested on either side of her, and the engagement ring sat on her left hand. She still hadn't taken it off—just as she promised me.

"When you go home, I'll go home." I turned back to the TV.

"Diesel," she repeated. "You're exhausted. Please go get some sleep."

"This couch is perfectly fine."

She sighed under her breath, her patience waning. "Thorn left."

"He's not your fiancé." We weren't married yet, but I already saw myself as her husband. If she was bedridden in the hospital, so was I. "I am."

She rolled her eyes.

I caught it in my peripheral, so I turned back to her, my eyes narrowed on her face. "Don't test me, baby." She might be on her way to recovery, but I was still on edge. Until I saw her strength returned to her and she was walking around on her stilettos, I would constantly be concerned.

A knock sounded on the open door. "Can I come in?" My father stood in black jeans and a long-sleeve dark blue shirt. It was a Tuesday, so he'd obviously skipped the office that afternoon.

Titan sat up higher in bed and smiled. "Please."

I'd asked my family to stay away so Titan wouldn't be overwhelmed. They'd done as I asked, but they couldn't do it forever.

My father walked into the room and stopped at her bedside. "You look good, Tatum."

"Thanks, Vincent."

He leaned down and kissed her on the cheek.

If he'd done that a month ago, I would have punched him in the face. But I knew he saw her as a daughter, and she saw him as a father.

He rested his hand on hers. "How are you feeling?"

"Good," Titan answered. "With every passing day, I feel a little stronger. The doctors said my tests are looking good, and I'm on my way to a full recovery. It'll just take me some time to get there."

"Knowing you, you'll do it in half the time." He squeezed her hand as he gave her a smile.

She smiled back. "I hope so."

He pulled his hand away and placed it in his pocket. He turned his gaze to me. "You look tired, son."

He called me that every chance he got. It was starting to become a habit I was getting used to remarkably fast. We went from not speaking for a decade to finding a relationship almost instantly. It was strange how normal it felt. "I'm fine."

Titan shook her hand. "I've asked him to go home and get some sleep, but he's very stubborn."

My father chuckled. "He's definitely the most stubborn son of the three."

I liked how he referred to Brett as one of us.

"I could have told you that," Titan said. "He hasn't eaten or showered."

"I'm fine," I repeated, annoyed that this was still a conversation.

Titan rolled her eyes at my father.

"I saw that," I said threateningly.

"Well, I made it pretty obvious," Titan countered.

My father chuckled at our banter. "Diesel, go home and get some sleep. I'll stay with Titan until you come back."

I stared at my father, unsure what to say.

He slid his hands into his pockets. "I'll watch her like a guard dog. I promise."

"Go, Diesel," Titan said. "I'm in good hands."

I rose from the couch and stood over Titan, my eyes on my father. "You would do that?"

"Of course." He wore a soft expression, but he still looked powerful in the way he held his thick frame.

"I know you're busy, Dad," I said. "You've got more important things to do."

He shook his head. "Nothing is more important than family, Diesel. I'd love to spend time with my future daughter-in-law."

My father was one of the most powerful men in this city—and the world. He could make anything happen with the snap of his fingers. He was frighteningly intelligent and built like an ox. No one would cross him—so they wouldn't cross her. There was no better company she could have. The only other person I would leave her with was Thorn, but he was catching up on missed sleep. I turned back to Titan. "Are you okay with that, baby?"

"Yes," she said irritably. "Now, go. I'll see you later."

"I'll be back in a few hours." I leaned down and kissed her.

She kissed me back longer than I expected, her kiss slightly sensual. "You'd better not be back in less than twelve hours. Otherwise, I won't let you through the door." She kissed the corner of my mouth before she let me pull away.

I rested my hand on hers, my thumb touching her ring. "Then I'll be back in twelve hours and one minute."

"And not a second sooner." She gave me that look of love I adored, the one that said I was the only man in the world that mattered. I'd never seen her look at anyone that way. Even when she was engaged to Thorn and putting on a show, she never gave him that expression. Only me. "I love you."

"I love you too." I'd never appreciated that exchange more. I had been afraid I would never get the chance to tell her those three little words again. Now I got to say them, and I had the rest of our lives to say them. "Call me if you need anything."

"Okay."

I walked around the bed then stopped in front of my father. "Don't leave her side, alright?"

He could have made a joke about my ridiculous protectiveness, but he didn't. Bruce was gone and she had no other enemies out there, but that didn't mean she was safe. I wanted someone to watch her at all times until she was healthy enough to look after herself again. "You have my word, son."

4
———

TITAN

THE TV PLAYED on the wall, but I didn't spend any time watching it. I wanted to ask someone to retrieve my laptop so I could get some work done, but I knew if Diesel found out, he would flip. He'd been through a lot, and I didn't want to push him.

Vincent sat on the couch next to my bedside, his arm resting over the back of it. His eyes were on the TV most of the time, and the comfortable silence stretched between us just the way it did between Thorn and me.

Diesel had been gone for about five hours, and I knew he'd fallen asleep the second his head hit the pillow. He hid exhaustion from me well, but I knew he was slowly falling apart. He hadn't eaten or showered since I'd been admitted to the hospital four days ago. He slept on and off when I slept during the night, but that would make even the strongest man buckle under the stress.

I was glad he finally took some time for himself.

"Need anything, Tatum?" Vincent asked.

"No, thank you. I'm fine." I was still propped up in bed, a large window to my right. I could see the whole city from my floor. It was a nice view, reminding me of the view from my penthouse.

"My son really loves you." He turned his gaze on me, his dark brown eyes identical to Diesel's. "The whole time we were in the waiting room, he could barely talk. He was a mess. I've never seen my son so scared in my life. Losing his mother was hard for him, but this was of a whole new caliber."

I knew how much Diesel had been hurting. I didn't need to see him suffer to understand. All I had to do was imagine the situation reversed, and I understood completely. "I know he does…"

He turned back to the TV.

"Things seem to be going well with the two of you."

"Yeah, they are," he said. "I'm grateful. I'm glad I got to sit there in the waiting room with him. I'm grateful I had the privilege to comfort him, to be there for him when he needed someone most. I'm grateful I got to be a father to him...after all the time I lost."

"I am too."

"Thanks to you," he said quietly. "Perhaps my wife won't be as angry with me when I see her again..."

She'd been gone for nearly ten years, but he still worshiped her like their love hadn't dwindled in their separation. "She won't be angry with you, Vincent. You've more than made up for everything."

He wore a small smile, but it only lasted an instant. "I hope you're right, Tatum." He changed his position on the couch and faced me, one leg crossed. It was five in the evening, and Diesel wouldn't be back until much later. "So, do you have any ideas for the wedding?"

"I haven't given it much thought."

"How about you give it some thought now?"

"Well...I know I want something small. Just us and a few other people."

He nodded.

"Somewhere that we won't be photographed like crazy. Maybe in France."

"France is beautiful."

"All I want is to wear a wedding dress. Everything else doesn't matter to me."

"You'll be a beautiful bride, Tatum—no matter what you wear."

"Thanks, Vincent."

"I look forward to it. When do you think this is going to happen?"

"As soon as possible."

"Yeah?" he asked in surprise.

I hadn't even asked Diesel, but I knew he wanted the same thing I did. "As soon as I'm back on my feet, I want to be husband and wife. I don't want to wait around, not knowing what's going to happen. My day was completely ordinary when I got shot. We think we have an entire lifetime, but we really don't know how much time we have."

"Very true," he said. "It was an ordinary day when my wife was taken from me. I continue to replay that day over and over in my mind. If I'd just asked her to stay, it never would have happened. She would be here now. She would see her son get married to a wonderful woman." Whenever he spoke of his wife, it was always full of sorrow, but it also lacked emotion at the same time. He accepted her death, but he didn't accept his life without her. "Just the way Diesel feels about you. If he'd been there...maybe things would have been different. I'm glad the outcome for him was much different than it was for me."

"I'm so sorry, Vincent..."

"I know you are, Titan." He sat perfectly straight in his chair, his broad shoulders still carrying the power of someone in their youth. Despite his obvious power, he couldn't protect himself from the painful sting of loss.

"You know, you're still very young, Vincent."

The corner of his mouth rose in a smile. "Thank you, Titan. I certainly don't feel like a man in his late fifties."

"You could live another forty years."

"I hope I do. Grandchildren are something I'm looking forward to."

I smiled. "But there could be a lot more to look forward to...if you had someone to share your life with." I didn't want to push Vincent to do anything he didn't want to do, but he was a handsome man who still had a lot to offer. He had another chance at happiness—if he wanted it. "I'm not trying to offend you—"

"You never offend me, sweetheart."

My train of thought immediately seized when he used the endearment. My father used to call me that every single day. Thorn called me that from time to time, but it felt different coming from Vincent, a man I viewed as a father figure. "I just wonder if you could be happy again if you gave it another chance. I'm sure your wife would want you to find someone else."

"I know she would," he said simply. "But I don't know…"

I didn't want to push him, not when it wasn't my place. If I lost Diesel, I probably wouldn't be interested in love again either. It took me nearly ten years just to give a man a chance in the first place. "You don't have to force it, but maybe keep the door open." He spent time with women my age, women who probably only wanted him for his money. If he started dating someone closer in age, he might find a genuine connection.

"I'll think about it. But I've been alone for so long that I'm not even sure how to be with someone. My flings only last a few months at a time…and I always tell them it's just a fling and nothing more."

"Just keep an open mind…and maybe look for someone your age."

"Most of the women my age are married."

"Not all."

He turned his gaze back to the TV. "Can I ask you something personal?"

"Yes."

"You don't have to answer it if you don't want to."

"I know." I felt comfortable with Vincent quickly. Even if he weren't Diesel's father, I'd feel some kind of affection for him. He was a gentleman, a strong man with a sensitive soul. He didn't need to be ruthless all the time to command respect.

"How did it feel...to be shot?" He watched me with his strong gaze, but his eyes were slightly squinted with hesitance. "Like I said, you don't have to answer."

I didn't feel any stress from the trauma. It was a chaotic event, but I conquered it and moved past it. I wasn't afraid of being gunned down again. When the gun was pointed in my face, I didn't flinch. I didn't give in either. I fought to the very end—and I won. "It wasn't painful. My body must have been in such a state of shock that I couldn't even feel it. When I lost my blood, I didn't feel that either. My pulse pounded in my ears, and I didn't even have time to think. I just knew I had to survive and I was going to do anything to make that happen. So I did what I had to do...and I don't feel bad about it."

"You shouldn't. He deserved it."

"I don't have any nightmares about it. Firing that

gun gave me closure. Now I know my biggest enemy is gone, and I sleep well."

"I'm glad that's how you feel. And thank you for answering my question."

"Sure."

"I wish I could kill the guy who killed my wife… but he's rotting in jail for the rest of his life. I suppose that's good enough."

There was no amount of retribution that would ever console him for his loss, but it was better than nothing. "I'm glad you got justice."

"Yeah…"

A knock sounded on the door, and Thorn walked inside. He was in a new suit, and his hair was styled after a shower. He looked a lot better than the last time I saw him, when he was sleep-deprived and dirty. "Can I come in?"

"You can always come in," I answered.

He came to my bedside and rested his hand on my arm. "How are you feeling? You're looking good."

"Thanks. I definitely feel better."

"Color is coming back to your cheeks. You're smiling. You look like the old you."

"Thanks."

He turned to Vincent. "Hey, how are you?"

"Good," Vincent answered. "Just spending some time with Tatum."

Thorn glanced at the bathroom door, which was open, and then turned back to me. "Where's Diesel?"

"He went home," I said. "He needed to get some sleep and take a shower."

"Wow," Thorn said. "I'm surprised he left."

"Tatum had to make him," Vincent said. "And I offered to watch her."

"Oh...makes sense." Thorn smiled at me. "I figured he wouldn't leave your side unless he was forced to."

"He's a bit dramatic sometimes," I said with a chuckle.

"He is dramatic," Thorn said in agreement. "But he's also a good guy—the best."

I smiled. "Thanks, Thorn."

He pulled his hand away. "Can I bring you anything from the outside world?"

"An Old Fashioned," I answered.

He shook his head. "Nice try."

"Then I don't need anything," I said. "I have everything I need."

"How much longer are you going to be in here?" He placed both of his hands in the pockets of his suit.

"At least five more days...unfortunately." I couldn't wait to go home. At least I could get some work done while I was in bed.

"My parents want to stop by tomorrow. Is that okay?"

"Of course it is. I would love to see them."

"They've been pretty worried about you," Thorn said. "When I told them you were going to be alright, my mom cried for ten minutes."

"Aww...she's so sweet."

"My dad is relieved too. You're like a daughter to them."

They'd always made me feel that way. "I know..."

He pulled a deck of cards out of his pocket. "You wanna play a round of poker?"

He and I used to play whenever we tried to kill time on the plane. "Thorn, I know you're busy. Just stopping by and saying hello is more than enough."

He pulled up a chair and situated the table in between us. "Just because we aren't getting married doesn't mean we aren't family. So there's no place in the world I'd rather be than here with you."

5

THORN

I KNEW Titan well enough to understand how important work was to her.

She gave workaholic a whole new definition.

It wasn't about money. It was about respect and power. She needed to keep her status as the richest woman in the world because of the prestige it provided her. It changed the landscape of female empowerment, and she took it upon herself to be that champion.

I understood all of her businesses because I'd watched them grow from the ground up. So I was the best one to manage them in her absence. I didn't tell her what I was doing before I did it. Knowing her, she would tell me not to worry about it because I had my own businesses to handle.

So I would just do it anyway.

I went to her main office, which was just a few blocks from her penthouse. I checked in with Jessica at the front and told her I would be running the company in Titan's absence. She didn't bother checking with Titan because she knew I had the authority to do it.

It would make more sense for Diesel to be handling this since he was marrying her. But I knew he didn't care about work right now.

Titan was the only thing he cared about.

I sat in her elegant office, a new vase of flowers on the corner of the desk even though she wasn't there. The white wood of her desk was smooth to the touch, and her white Mac sat exactly where she'd left it. The gray couches on the white rug comple-mented the matching walls on either side. Her office looked more like a living room in a Pottery Barn catalogue.

She had great taste.

I answered her emails, looked through the reports that came across her desk, rearranged her schedule, and handled her meetings.

Jessica knocked before she walked inside. "Titan has a meeting with Ms. Alexander in thirty minutes."

I looked away from the screen and gave her my

attention. Jessica was a young redhead, someone Titan described as amateur but full of potential. From the strong way she carried herself and her eloquence, she'd obviously grown a lot working under a powerful woman like Titan. Now her confidence was unmistakable. "What is it regarding?"

"Ms. Alexander owns one of the biggest solar companies in the country. She specializes in green and renewable energy, and I believe Titan is interested in buying her out, but I'm not completely sure. Since Titan is unavailable right now, perhaps I should reschedule."

This wasn't as straightforward. I could handle the meeting, but I needed to know exactly what Titan wanted before I acted on her behalf. It would be wrong to take charge of the situation when it wasn't clear. "Let me call her."

"Alright." Jessica walked out.

I called Diesel.

He answered immediately. "Hey, what's up?"

"How's she doing today?"

"She's good. Ate all of her breakfast."

"Because you made her?" I teased.

Diesel didn't rise to my humor. As long as she sat in that hospital bed, Diesel wouldn't be in a good mood. "Maybe. Are you coming by?"

"Actually, I need to talk to her. Can you put her on?"

"Hold on." Diesel transferred the phone to Titan.

She spoke with her deep and powerful voice. "Hey, Thorn. What's going on?"

"Long story short, I've been taking care of stuff for you at the office."

"You have?" she asked in surprise.

"I know you've been thinking about work the whole time you've been in that bed. Let's not pretend otherwise."

Her long pause was a confirmation of my accusation. "Well, that's not all I've been thinking about. But you didn't need to do that, Thorn. I appreciate it more than I can say...but you still didn't need to worry about it."

"I don't mind. You would do the same for me."

"Of course." She was obviously touched by what I'd done. When she said very little, her stretches of silence spoke louder than words. "I know you have your own company to take care of. I'll be back on my feet soon. I always have Diesel too."

"Don't worry about it. I can handle it. Diesel shouldn't have to worry about it either."

"Well...thank you."

"No problem. But I do have a question."

"Fire away."

"I have a meeting with someone named Alexander in, like, twenty minutes. Apparently, she has a solar company you're interested in. I know you're expanding your projects in solar energy, but I'm not sure what you want from this person."

Titan immediately switched into her executive role. "I want to buy her out. Offer whatever is necessary to acquire it. With her technology and expertise, I know I'll be able to grow my company exponentially and be the leading solar technology company in the country. I'll be able to monopolize the market. Ms. Alexander is a brilliant woman who's not only scientifically inclined, but she has a strong business presence. Don't underestimate her."

"She shouldn't underestimate me either. But are you certain you don't want to reschedule and handle this yourself?"

She paused as she considered it. "I won't be out of here for a few more days, and even then, I'll probably be in bed for a while. I don't think it's the best time for me to handle such a big task, but I also don't want to put it off either. I have no doubt you can handle this. I've learned everything from the best— and the best is you."

I couldn't stop the smile from spreading across my face. "Alright. I'll bring this home for you."

"Thank you, Thorn. But remember what I said, don't underestimate her."

"Have you met her?"

"No," Titan answered. "But her reputation precedes her."

———

JESSICA SPOKE THROUGH THE INTERCOM. "MR. Cutler, Ms. Alexander has arrived."

"Send her in." I was familiar with Titan's projects and goals. She viewed solar energy as the future of all business. By converting to a power source that didn't cost money, she would cut her business expenses all over the world. Her entire buildings were going to run on the new form of energy, which wouldn't cost her a dime. According to her books, it would save her nearly ten million dollars every year. By making the energy source more affordable, it would be an incentive for other businesses to convert. If she were the only company in power, she would get all the business—from the entire world. She'd even convinced me to change all my offices and factories to solar, and that construction would begin soon.

Jessica opened the glass door and allowed Ms. Alexander inside.

The second she stepped into the office, I couldn't hide my surprise.

She was not what I pictured—at all.

I'd expected a middle-aged woman, someone who wore glasses to go along with her nerdy appearance. I didn't expect her to have any confidence or social skills at all. But the woman I saw looked nothing like that.

She was young.

Younger than me.

She had jet-black hair, which was long and thick. It reached just past her perky tits. Her pink blouse fit snugly around her chest, stretching slightly over the womanly curves. The blouse hugged her slender waistline, curving inward until it disappeared under her skirt at her hips. A gold necklace was around her throat, a circular pendant in the center.

Her black skirt reached just above her knee, hinting at her toned legs underneath the fabric. Her heels were sky-high, but she handled them like sandals on the soft sand of some beach. She held a folder in one arm, a rose gold watch sitting around her wrist.

She stopped at my desk, staring at me like she wasn't nearly as surprised to see me as I was to see her.

I forgot to rise from my chair, thrown off by the gorgeous woman who had just stepped inside the office like she owned it. I got to my feet, straightened my tie, and stared at her face without blinking. In fact, I hadn't blinked once since she'd walked into the office. There was too much to look at.

She extended her hand and wore a soft smile on her lips. It wasn't the wide and flirtatious one women sometimes flashed my way, the kind that was so big it compensated for their nervousness. Hers was absolutely confident, indifferent to my opinion of her. "Mr. Cutler, it's a pleasure."

The second my fingers touched her soft skin, I imagined placing my lips along the tender spots of her wrist. I wanted to feel her pulse with my mouth, to feel every slight reaction she gave at my touch. My fingers latched on to her hand, and she gave me as firm a shake as I gave her.

The second our hands broke apart, the images faded from my mind. I saw beautiful women every day, so Ms. Alexander shouldn't impress me. She was certainly stunning, but not the most beautiful woman in the world. I turned off my attraction the instant it occurred, knowing this was only about business. She had something that I wanted—and I was going to get it from her. "The pleasure is mine, Ms. Alexander. Have a seat."

She sat in the cushioned armchair in front of the desk, a chair that was far too comfortable for a business meeting. All the furniture in my own office was wooden because I didn't want anyone to stay for too long. "I hope Ms. Titan is doing alright. I've seen the news."

"She'll make a full recovery."

"I'm glad to hear that." She crossed her legs and rested her folder on her lap. "And it's nice of you to help her out."

"Of course. She's my..." I trailed away when I realized I couldn't say what I wanted to say. I had to pretend she was my ex-fiancé, a woman I'd loved and lost. I had to keep up the pretense to this woman, even though she must find it strange that I was there. "It's no problem."

Ms. Alexander maintained the same expression, her thick lips painted red with her lipstick. She had thick eyelashes, olive skin, and she possessed self-assuredness no matter what her position was. She wasn't afraid to make eye contact with me. Stretches of silence didn't seem to bother her either. Most importantly, my solid stare didn't unnerve her either.

I was the one with the agenda, so I started the conversation. "Ms. Titan is impressed with your innovative work. Your work with solar energy is nothing short of remarkable. You've made tremendous leaps in such a short amount of time."

"Thank you. That's a compliment coming from someone like her."

I wanted to ask how old she was, but since it was rude and irrelevant, I didn't. Just because she was young didn't mean her achievements were questionable. I could probably find all my answers once I Googled her after she left. I hadn't had the forethought to do it before. "Titan thinks your company would aid her own work with solar energy."

"I know it would."

Perhaps this acquisition would be easier than I thought. Maybe Ms. Alexander wanted to be bought out. She'd made her fortune, and she would get another fortune from Titan. She could retire and live out her life quietly—and very comfortably. "Which is why she's prepared to buy your company—and make you a handsome offer."

It was the first time her expression changed. The

soft smile evaporated from her lips, and her green eyes slightly narrowed on my face. She didn't hide her displeasure at my words, being utterly transparent with me. "I'm not interested in selling my company."

Then what did she think this meeting was for? "If you aren't interested in selling, what are you interested in?"

"A partnership."

That answer told me everything I needed to know. My first impression of her was completely wrong. She wasn't the simple type, the kind of woman who just wanted her money and a comfortable life. She was ambitious, driven, and fierce. She wanted more than just her company. She wanted to grow, and she was looking for a powerful partner to help her get there. This was just the beginning for her. She had her entire life ahead of her, and she wanted to make her mark on the world. It made me respect her more. "Your ambition is respectable. Titan is the richest woman in the world because she never stopped. She grew one company then started another. There's a lot you can learn from her. But she's not looking for a partnership. I suggest you take her offer and walk away a very rich woman." I grabbed the notepad, scribbled down the offer, and then pushed it toward her across the desk.

She didn't even glance at it. Her gaze was focused on me, a natural light burning in her eyes. They had a gentle smolder, a fire of ferocity that she didn't let kindle. It was a controlled burn because she was completely in control of her emotions. "My company isn't for sale."

She was either very brave or very stupid. She had no idea how much money was on the table. Titan wasn't the kind of person to lowball people. She had a strict code of ethics, and she'd never been interested in getting ahead by ripping people off—especially another woman. "I suggest you look at the offer before you turn it down."

"There's not enough money in the world to make me change my mind."

Damn.

"I want a partnership with Titan. I'm the engineer of most of my products. I have a big vision for the future of renewable energy. I'm interested in changing the world, making a difference for all of humanity, not filling my bank account with more money than I'll ever need. I need Titan to help me grow, for us both to be extremely rich, and for both of us to change the world. The one thing I don't need is her money—I have plenty of that."

My hand immediately gripped the armrest of the chair, not because I was irritated, but because I found her directness sexy. There were lots of women working in corporate America, but none like this. Not only was she beautiful, but she knew exactly what she wanted. She liked money just as much as the rest of us, but she also wasn't obsessed with it. She knew her worth, and Titan would respect her for it.

But Titan had her own interests—and I had to protect them. "I respect your decision, but I won't change mine. As much as Titan is interested in your engineering, she's interested in being the sole enterprise in this country. Take the money, make a counteroffer, or walk out as her competitor. But let me warn you...you don't want to be her competitor."

Ms. Alexander didn't shift her position in her chair. With a straight posture and poised shoulders, she held herself like a queen. If a tiara were on her head, it would be sitting perfectly straight. Her tanned skin looked great with that pink blouse, and the classy watch on her wrist gave her another touch of elegance. She had the most beautiful poker face I'd ever seen, and now she used it against me. Her expression was no longer transparent, her thoughts an empty black hole of mystery.

My hand continued to grip my armrest, anticipating what she would say. Would she stick to her guns and walk away? Would she leave such a fortune sitting on the table? Or would she come to her senses and realize this was the best option she was ever going to get?

She broke the silence with her beautiful voice. "Thank you for your time, Mr. Cutler." She rose to her feet and approached my desk. "But I'm not interested in anything less than what I came here for."

.

6

DIESEL

I WALKED into the room at ten in the evening, refreshed from sleeping in my own bed and taking a hot shower. I carried the vase of lilies into the room and placed them on the table directly beside her bed.

The second Titan looked at them, her face lit up with excitement. "They're beautiful..."

I'd picked them up on my way home, and I knew they would liven up her hospital room. There was nothing she loved more than a fresh vase of flowers. They were always in her office and always in her home.

"Lilies..."

"Your favorite, I know."

She sat up in bed, that usual look of adoration in her eyes. "How did you know?"

The corner of my mouth rose in a smile as I walked to the bed. "Because I know you better than anyone." I leaned down and kissed her on the mouth, feeling my heart speed up the second my lips were connected to hers. My father was still there, but I didn't care. I'd almost lost her, and I was going to kiss her whenever the hell I felt like it. I rubbed my nose against hers before I pulled away. "How are you?"

"Good. Your father kept me company all day."

My father rose from the couch and patted me on the back. "Don't worry, I didn't tell her too many embarrassing stories."

"Better not," I threatened.

He leaned down and kissed her on the cheek. "I'll see you later, sweetheart."

"Bye, Vincent."

My father walked out and shut the door behind him.

I noticed how close Titan and my father had become over the last few months. They seemed to have their own relationship, their own connection. Most of the time, it didn't seem like it had anything to do with me. Even if I weren't the connection between them, they would still be compatible. "How was your day?"

"Good. Thorn came by in the morning. Some of my friends stopped by too."

"A lot of visitors then?"

"Yeah. It was nice."

I walked to the couch on the other side of the bed and took a seat.

"Thorn has been helping me with work. He called me from the office today. He's been running the show for the past few days."

That didn't surprise me. "That was nice of him."

"I know," she said with a sigh. "He's a good guy."

"I don't know about that. I just think he loves you."

She smiled. "Yeah, true."

I moved to the edge of the bed and took a seat, just so I could be close to her. My fingers found hers, and I looked into her pretty face. She hadn't been wearing makeup for a while, but I preferred the look. I liked it when she was most vulnerable, when she opened up her entire heart to me. "Any news from the doctor?"

"They're still observing me."

"How's the pain?"

"Excruciating when the medication wears off," she said with a chuckle. "But I do feel better, overall."

"You look good." My hand moved into her hair, and I gently brushed some strands away from her face.

"You're sweet."

"I mean it." My fingers trailed down her arm to her elbow. "Anything I can get you?"

"You already brought everything I could possibly need—flowers and you."

My look intensified. It was impossible for me not to stare at her possessively, no matter what the context was. "I can't wait until you're better."

"Why?"

"Because I can't wait to marry you."

Her eyes softened the second the words were out of my mouth.

I leaned in and kissed her on the mouth, feeling the comfort only her lips could bring. When we were connected like this, I forgot she was in a hospital room. I forgot everything she'd been through—everything I'd been through. It was just us, and that told me everything would be okay.

"Is this a bad time?" Thorn walked in, his feet tapping against the tile floor.

I didn't pull away from her out of principal. I took another second to finish my kiss before I pulled back. I got off the bed and faced him. "Come in, Thorn."

In a navy blue suit and a matching tie, he approached Titan's bed. Both hands rested in his pockets. "Since you guys are always kissing, I guess it's always a bad time." He looked at the vase at her bedside. He probably figured out they were from me because he never asked. "I know it's late, but I just wanted to stop by before I turned in for the night."

She grabbed his arm and gave it a squeeze. "I'm always happy to see you, Thorn—even if I'm kissing my fiancé at the time."

"You say that now, but when you're back at home, you'll feel differently," he said with a chuckle.

I sat on the couch wearing jeans and a t-shirt. I knew Titan would be going to sleep soon, and I would stay awake most of the night watching the silent TV or looking at her. But I'd much rather be beside her than anywhere else in the world.

"How'd it go with Ms. Alexander?"

He stared at her for a moment before he released a quiet sigh. "Not well."

Titan never panicked in any situation. She could be losing all of her businesses, but she would still remain calm. I'd only seen her lose her temper once—and it was justified. Even when a gun was pointed at her face, she thought logically to solve the problem. That was one of the reasons she was the powerhouse she was now. "What happened?"

"I made the offer, but she wouldn't look at it. She said she only wants a partnership—not your money."

"What else did she say?"

"That's it," Thorn said. "The conversation was short. I told her to reconsider, but she refused. Then she got up and left."

Titan turned to the TV, her face stoic as she considered everything she'd just learned. Her lips pressed together tightly, her chest rising and falling at the same pace. "I would talk to her myself, but I'm in no condition."

"Honestly, I don't think even you could change her mind, Titan. This woman…" He shook his head slightly as he thought about it. "She knows exactly what she wants. She's not going to change her mind. We either have to fold or let her walk away."

She turned back to him. "Thorn, everything I've learned I've learned from you."

He held her gaze, his blue eyes unblinking.

"Change her mind, Thorn," she said. "Offer her more money."

"How can I offer her more when she wouldn't even look?" he questioned.

"Then you don't make her look," she countered. "You tell her the number. Then you keep going up until she changes her mind. I need her business in order for this to be a success. Unless I acquire her or run her out of business, my goals will never be reached. She's reputed to be one of the brightest scientists of our generation. I need her to cave, Thorn."

He held his impassive gaze, listening to her without giving anything in return.

"I've already invested billions into this company," Titan said. "This is the second piece I need for complete domination."

Thorn didn't move. "Having a partnership is out of the question?"

"I don't do partnerships," she said firmly. "You know that."

His eyes moved to my face before they turned back to her.

"That's different," she countered. "He's going to be my husband. He's the one exception."

I couldn't help but smile at the way she referred to me. Her one exception.

"I'll talk to her again," Thorn said. "But I'm

telling you, this woman is different. You haven't seen her. You don't know what she's like. Honestly, she reminds me a lot of you. She's tiny, but her presence takes up the whole room. She knows what she wants, and she won't settle for less. For her, it's not about money. It's about making a difference. I think this is a battle you won't win."

She stared at him, her gaze hardening just the way it did when she was in a meeting. "Then you win it for me, Thorn."

———

THE NEXT THREE DAYS PASSED BY SLOWLY.

I was anxious for the doctor to give her permission to go home. Not only did I want her all to myself, but I wanted the final obstacle to be overcome. If the doctor said she was free to go home, then that meant she was truly okay.

We would get through this.

The worst of it was over.

"Diesel."

I loved hearing her voice, no matter what she was saying. She could speak in a different language, and I would enjoy just listening to her. It wasn't just the deep and sexy sound of her voice; it was the fact that she was the woman I loved. No one else could soothe me the way she could. Every day we were in that hospital room, she was the one comforting me —not the other way around. "Yes, baby?" I turned my gaze on her, seeing her sit with the sheets pulled to her waist.

"You should get to the office today. I know you have stuff to do." She constantly pressured me to go back to work, to get back to my regular routine because the work was piling up. All my meetings were rescheduled, and everything I'd been working on was halted.

"I couldn't care less about work, baby." I hadn't thought about it once since this tragedy had happened. All I cared about was the woman beside me. Money didn't matter to me anymore, not when I had this brilliant diamond in my life.

"Diesel, I'm going to be okay. I'm going home tomorrow."

"Doesn't matter. As long as you're in here, I'm in here too."

Her eyes tightened with emotion, and a small smile stretched across her lips. "You're sweet, Diesel. But you really don't have to stay with me."

"I know I don't have to." I looked into her beautiful green eyes, getting lost in their vibrant color. I loved staring at them every morning and every night. They were beacons that guided me to happiness every single day. "I want to."

———————

HER TEAM OF DOCTORS FINALLY GAVE HER PERMISSION to be discharged from the hospital. She was still on pain medication, along with a serious strain of antibiotics. She wouldn't need physical therapy because her injury hadn't jeopardized her mobility. But she was still required to get lots of rest, to spend most of her time in bed, and schedule follow-up visits to monitor the wound in her chest.

She still had a long road ahead of her until she was back to normal, but everything would be easy in comparison to what she'd already been through. My woman was the strongest and fiercest one in the entire world. She killed the man who attempted to murder her. I had no doubt she could get through this.

My woman was a badass.

I got her back to her penthouse, and she didn't have an issue walking. If she was in pain, she purposely didn't show it. She walked a little slower than usual, and when we stepped inside the lobby of her building, she purposely looked at the spot where she'd hit the floor after she'd been shot.

After a short pause, she kept walking.

We rode the elevator to the top floor and then stepped inside her apartment. It was exactly the way she'd left it, her heels next to the couch along with a glass of scotch. The ice had melted long ago, and now it was just a watered-down drink.

I hoped her home wasn't too close to her trauma. I hoped she could feel safe here, that her sanctuary hadn't been ruined by Bruce Carol. "We can go to my place if you'd prefer." We would have to choose a place to live together anyway. My place was similar to hers, about the same size. Or we could pick a whole new place altogether and start over.

"This is fine." She hit the lights, dimming them to her desired level. She looked around at her penthouse, taking it in like it was the first time she'd ever truly looked at it. She placed her hand against the wall and felt the smoothness. "I thought I would never see this place again..." She walked into her bedroom.

I followed behind her and joined her in the large bedroom.

She slowly pulled off her clothes, the change of clothes I had brought to the hospital. It was a t-shirt and sweatpants, and she slowly stripped everything away.

I got on my knees and helped her undress, knowing she was unsteady even though she refused to show it. When she was in just her panties, I tried not to look at her in a way I shouldn't. But my lips couldn't be controlled, and I pressed a kiss to the inside of her thigh. I quickly turned my face away and stood upright, pushing the thought from my mind. Even with the enormous gauze wrapped around her chest, covering her wound and her tits, I still thought the naked sight of her was undeniably arousing. "How about I make you something to eat?"

"I'm not hungry. But thank you." She looked at me with her pretty face, her cheeks a little more hollow because she seemed to have lost some weight. The color had returned to her cheeks, and the affection in her eyes was undeniable. The second I'd kissed her inner thigh, the same thoughts had come into her mind.

I grabbed one of my t-shirts from the drawer and pulled it over her lithe body. I covered her beautiful skin, her toned stomach and her sexy hips. My fingers couldn't resist touching her panties, so I moved them across the band before I pulled them away.

"Could you grab my laptop?" she asked. "It's my bag in the living room."

I knew exactly what she wanted it for. "No."

Her eyebrow immediately rose. "Excuse me?"

"No working."

She flashed me an incredulous look. "Diesel, I have a lot to catch up on."

"Yes—your health." I turned away from her and pulled my shirt over my head before I tossed it in the laundry basket. "That's all you should be focusing on." I pulled a t-shirt out of my drawer and pulled it over my head. When I turned back to her, her eyes were erupting with lava.

"Let's get something straight, Diesel. You don't tell me what to do, whether you're my husband or not."

"Actually, I do. And you'll do the same for me when I need to hear it."

Her anger didn't dim.

"Thorn is taking care of the office, so there's nothing for you to do anyway."

"There's always something for me to do. Thorn has his own work to handle."

"He wouldn't offer if he couldn't handle it. This discussion is over." I dropped my jeans and placed them in the basket.

Now she looked terrifying. Her eyes narrowed on my face like she was about to take me down. "This discussion isn't over just because you say it is. If you want to marry me, you're going to have to—"

I shut her up with a kiss. I wrapped my hands around her waist, and I pressed my mouth to hers. I kissed her slowly, my lips feeling hers sensually. I breathed into her mouth; she breathed back. Our mouths fell into place, and we embraced each other slowly. My tongue moved into her mouth and was immediately greeted by her own. I slipped my hand into her hair, and I deepened the kiss. Out of my control, my cock hardened, and I pictured her on her back, her legs open around my waist as she moaned with every thrust I gave her. My sexual desire wasn't lustful in nature. I just missed being with her, being connected in the most intimate way possible. I'd asked her to be my wife and I'd made love to her for the rest of the night, but then the following day, everything changed.

I ended the embrace before I lost my self-control altogether. "No fighting. We've been through too much to fight." I rubbed my nose against hers and stared at the calmness in her eyes. "I know you aren't the kind of woman who can be bossed around. It's one of the reasons I want to marry you. But we're in a different circumstance right now. We need to focus on getting you better. Work is just work. It'll still be there when you get back."

TITAN DROPPED THE FIGHT AND DIDN'T REVISIT IT again. She took it easy as I asked, spending her time watching old classics like *I Love Lucy*. Showering was difficult because of her gauze. It had to be protected from the water, so I covered her with a waterproof garbage bag.

Seeing her naked didn't help my restraint.

I worked from the penthouse, taking care of most things with my assistants through email. I had meetings over the phone, using her home office so I could have the space and privacy. Going to the office would simplify everything, but I refused to leave her unattended. I stayed by her side every hour of the day, monitoring her health like I was her private physician.

I walked into the living room and saw her sitting on the couch with a blanket over her thighs. The TV was on and she watched it, but she didn't have the same vigor in her gaze that she usually possessed.

I leaned over the back of the couch and kissed

her on the shoulder. "Everything alright, baby?" I was shirtless and in just my sweatpants, the attire I wore around the house. I'd never been indoors for such a long time. I didn't even go to the gym. I tried to do some workouts at home, doing sit-ups and push-ups in the living room.

She leaned her back and looked up at me. "I'm not the kind of person who sits around and watches TV...not a fan of it."

"Just be patient."

She growled before she raised her head again. "I miss working..."

"I know." I kissed the back of her head.

"I miss fucking."

Immediately, my cock hardened in my boxers. It went to full mast surprisingly fast, breaking my best record. Sex was on my mind just as heavily. Sharing the same bed all night was pretty much torture. We used to make love every night before we went to sleep. Now, that routine was gone. "Everything will be back to normal soon." It took all my strength to say those words and not pin her to the couch and fuck her then and there. I stepped away from the couch and walked to the dining room table. My laptop was sitting there, so I opened it and got to work.

She turned around and looked at me over the back of the couch. "Diesel, you can go into the office. I'll call you if I need anything."

"Baby, I'm fine."

She sighed in annoyance. "I get you don't want me to work, but life goes on. You need to take care of your companies. If you think I'm gonna work the second you walk out, I won't. If I say I won't do something, I won't."

"That isn't why I want to stay home with you. You know that."

She turned back to the TV. "Alright...my offer is still on the table."

I spent the rest of the day working, and I made dinner toward the end of the night. We ate at the table together, and Titan stared at my chest without hiding the intent in her gaze. The drought between us was affecting her just as deeply as it was affecting me.

Maybe our restraint wouldn't last much longer.

When we got ready for bed, Titan took her clothes off instead of putting them on. She stood in front of me in just the gauze that was wrapped around her chest. She pushed her thong away and stared at me with a commanding gaze, telling me she was going to get what she wanted no matter how hard I fought it.

But I didn't want to fight it.

Her fingertips played with the strings of my sweatpants, and she yanked the knot free. Then she pushed my pants and my boxers down together until my rock-hard cock emerged. He was thicker than he'd ever been before, suffering from the deepest drought of his life. She pushed my boxers past my thighs, letting my balls come free too. "Diesel." She stepped closer to me, her lips nearly touching mine. Her fingertips cupped my balls and gently massaged them.

I let out an involuntary breath. Her warm fingers felt perfect against my balls, touching them exactly the way they should be touched.

"You're gonna make love to me. That's the end of the discussion."

I didn't want to say no, not when my balls felt so good in her fingertips. "I don't want to hurt you."

"You won't." She moved her lips to mine and kissed me slowly.

The second her mouth was on mine, I was gone.

"Be slow. Be gentle."

I moved my hand into her hair, and I deepened the kiss, my balls tightening in her hands. I wanted to sink between her legs, move through her slickness and enjoy that overwhelming tightness. I wanted to show my woman I loved her, fall into the deep abyss of intimacy. I wanted to enjoy her body, touch her soul.

Her hands wrapped around my shaft, and she gently stroked me, touching me better than I touched myself. She knew exactly what I liked, what touches ignited me into a frenzy. Any other woman could touch me the same way, but it wouldn't yield the same reaction. The only reason why I was so hot was because she was the woman I was hot for.

My woman.

I guided her to the bed then released her when the back of her knees hit the bed frame.

She guided herself back on the mattress, taking her time as she shifted her body up toward the headboard.

The second her back was against the sheets, I kicked off my bottoms and moved on top of her. My usually calm manner was gone now that my body was situated on top of hers. I'd been looking forward to this for over a week. Like I was a teenage boy and this was my first time, my hands slightly shook in anticipation.

My arms locked behind her knees, and I pinned

her legs back as I positioned myself between her legs.

Her hair was sprawled across the pillow around her, and her hands immediately reached for my biceps so she had something to grab on to. Her lips were slightly parted, her anticipation for my dick heavy.

I tilted my hips and pressed the head of my cock against her entrance. With a gentle shove, I pushed past her tightness and slowly sank into her.

She inhaled deeply, her eyes closing momentarily. "Diesel."

I pushed until my shaft was completely sheathed. I was surrounded by her wet tightness, by her lustful love. She wanted me like a fantasy, the ideal man that deserved her beautiful pussy. I held myself on top of her, most of my weight pressed on to my arms. I took slow breaths, feeling like a king now that I was finally inside her again. It felt so good that I didn't want to move. I looked into her face as I breathed, my eyes locked on to her heavy ones. The tops of her tits were noticeable, pressed together from the tightness of her gauze. Even when she was at her weakest point, I still found her to be the most desirable woman in the world. I loved everything about her, from the curve of her bottom lip to the hollow of her throat. She was gorgeous, inside and out.

My hips wanted to buck hard, but I stopped myself from taking her too roughly. I tightened my core and rocked my hips slowly, moving in and out of her with purposeful gentleness. I hardly rocked her at all, making sure I didn't move her more than necessary. "Baby..." I closed my eyes again as I enjoyed her. Even restrained lovemaking was the best sex I'd ever had. My cock felt right at home buried inside her, feeling my woman in the most intimate way possible.

"God..." Her hands moved to my chest, and her nails dug into me. She didn't rock her hips back into me like she usually did. She lay still, enjoying every inch of me. Her breathing was deep and heavy, and she moaned with every thrust I made. "Diesel...like that."

I craned my neck to hers, and I kissed her as I moved, doing my best to last as long as I could. The second the head of my cock was inside her, I wanted to dump all of my seed into her. I wanted to claim her as mine forever. The diamond ring was on her left hand, and I felt the warm metal against my skin as she pressed her palms into me.

Fuck, this felt incredible.

She stopped kissing me as her breathing took over. Her lips were still pressed to mine, but she was so overcome with moaning that she couldn't reciprocate anymore. She was on the edge of pleasure, about to fall into the powerful orgasm she'd begged me to give her.

I wanted to give it to her. "Come, baby."

That was the final touch she needed, and she came around me. She started to writhe, her body stretching and moving. She carved her nails into my skin, leaving marks over my pectoral muscles. "Diesel..."

She said my name more times than ever before, and I knew I was hitting her in the perfect spot. I watched the performance she gave, the way her mouth widened like she was singing a song. I listened to her moans as they turned into screams. I watched the way she stared at me like I was the only man in the world that mattered. There was no one before me, and there would be no one after me. I was all that mattered.

That made me feel like a king.

As soon as she finished, I dropped my restraint. I shoved my dick deep inside her and released with a grunt, feeling all the stress from the week fade away as I filled her pussy with everything I had. It was one of the best climaxes I'd ever had, and I knew it was just the beginning.

I'd thought I was going to lose her, but she was still there with me. She would be the mother of my children, the wife I would love every single day of my life. She would be a partner I would admire, even someone I would learn from. And I would be the king of her heart, the man she turned to for protection and strength. I would be everything she was missing in life.

And she would be everything I'd ever needed.

7

THORN

I PURPOSELY WAITED a few days to see if Ms. Alexander would reconsider the offer and return on her own.

But after the third day of silence, I knew she wasn't playing games.

She was dead serious.

When I warned Titan about this woman, she didn't take it seriously. She was the biggest shark in the ocean, so she wasn't intimidated by anyone.

I wasn't intimidated either. But how did you work with someone who wasn't motivated by money? She was motivated by something more meaningful. Now we were in a realm I didn't understand. Titan didn't understand it either.

But I knew how important this was to Titan, so I would make it happen. I may have to approach this woman in a different way, but that didn't matter. Whatever it took to get the job done was fine by me.

I was in Titan's office when I spoke to Jessica over the intercom. "Jessica, could you get Ms. Alexander on the phone for me?"

"Of course, sir. Hold on." She turned silent, and I finished writing the email I was working on. It didn't surprise me how many requests filled Titan's inbox. She was America's most famous person right now. There were lots of messages inquiring about her health. I responded to them as myself, just to give everyone a peace of mind. Titan would make a full recovery, and the most powerful woman in the world would be back on her feet in no time.

Jessica spoke again. "I have her for you. Line one."

"Thanks, Jessica." I picked up the phone and pressed it to my year. "Ms. Alexander." I typed her name into the search engine, and her page immediately popped up. There was a candid shot of her right on the first page, one of her walking to her private plane at JFK. In a black dress with sky-high heels, she approached the steps to board the plane. Aviator sunglasses sat on her nose, and her black hair was in spiral curls. Her calf muscles were impressive, but then again, everything about her was impressive. Drop-dead gorgeous and smart, she was a special kind of woman.

Her voice was heavy with confidence, but she didn't cross the line into arrogance. She had a special quality that made her innately endearing even though she was a powerhouse. She was aware of her power, but she didn't seem interested in throwing it anyone's face. Only someone secure in their success didn't care what others thought of them—and she was definitely secure. "Mr. Cutler, what a nice surprise. What can I do for you?"

Her sexy voice caught me off guard even though I'd already heard it. It fell on my ear at the perfect cadence, making me think of her mouth pressed right against the shell of my ear as I fucked her against the wall.

Why did I keep on thinking about fucking her?

She was just a pretty woman. Nothing more.

It was time to focus. "I'd like to have another discussion about your company. Let's set up a meeting in my office tomorrow." My fingers drummed against the white desk, focusing on the silence between us. I wanted to listen to her breathe, listen for the sound of apprehension. I couldn't gauge a single weakness when I met her in person. Now I was listening for it.

"I already came to your office and wasted my time. If you'd like to talk about this, you can make an appointment with my assistant."

My eyes flashed at the cold way she brushed me off. Like a queen full of indifference, she dismissed me as if I didn't mean anything to her. It was like a slap in the face. If anyone wanted to do business with me, they came at my beck and call. But this woman obviously operated under a different philosophy.

"Goodbye, Mr. Cutler." Without waiting for a response, she hung up on me.

Click.

I listened to the line go dead before I hung up the phone. I sat back in the chair, my fingertips resting across my lips. While I sat there rigid and silent, the emotions exploded inside me. No one had ever handled me so callously before. She was playing with fire, and she was about to get burned.

And I was so fucking hard.

I despised this woman, but my attraction didn't seem dependent on that fact. My mind and body had very different opinions about her. I didn't consider myself a proud man, but I did demand respect. I didn't care for the way she handled me. She should bend over backward for me like everyone else did. This deal didn't matter to me, so I didn't want to bother with the meeting. She could lose out on the opportunity, and I didn't give a damn about it.

But I gave a damn about Titan.

This was important to her.

If she were well enough, she would secure this deal. Perhaps she would have had better success since she was a woman, and Ms. Alexander would have responded to her very differently.

I told her I would make this happen, and I had to keep my word.

She was my best friend.

So I ground my teeth together before I spoke into the intercom. "Jessica, get me an appointment at Ms. Alexander's office."

***

ALEXANDER APPLICATIONS WASN'T IN THE CENTER OF Manhattan the way Titan's offices were. It was closer to the border and near the water's edge. A large, historic building sat at the front, designed with sensual and elegant features. Two stone horse statues stood at the entrance to the building. Behind the building was a large stone wall that enclosed the rest of the compound in the background. More buildings were in the distance, where the research was conducted.

The black-and-white tile entryway led to a spacious lobby that was elegant enough for a five-star hotel. Chandeliers hung from the ceiling, and its old-fashioned feel directed contradicted the new technology that was born out of this place.

I checked in at the front desk then took the elevator to the top floor. This area was vastly different than it was downstairs. Just like an Apple store, it was sleek, plain, and modern. The desks and chairs were constructed of a gray-blue material, and the walls were made of a dark hardwood. I checked in with another assistant and then was guided to a separate waiting room.

It was a big waiting area for a single person. It made me wonder how many meetings she had a day. I was offered refreshments, but I declined. I surveyed the area then looked at the glass doors that took up the entire left side of the space. They were completely reflective, allowing Ms. Alexander to see out but no one to see in.

I wondered if she was looking at me right now.

I couldn't believe I was sitting there waiting to be seen.

I didn't wait for anyone.

But yet, I was sitting on my ass waiting for her.

She was probably dragging it out on purpose, just to remind me that she was in the position of power this time.

I didn't like that one bit.

If I had my way, I would just forget this meeting altogether and spend all my time trying to bury her company. Even with her genius mind, I could still crush her business. The most popular products on the market weren't necessarily the best; they just had better marketing. And marketing was my strength. I could decimate all of her hard work overnight.

And I was tempted to do it.

But then Titan came into my mind again. She was home right now, still weak from the gunshot wound that nearly killed her. Diesel wouldn't allow her to work, so it was up to me to make this happen. If I could deliver her good news, it would make her suffering more bearable.

So I swallowed my distaste and continued to wait.

Finally, her assistant walked into the room. "Ms. Alexander will see you now."

About time. I'd been sitting there for almost

twenty minutes—and I wasn't late or early to the meeting.

The assistant opened the glass door and held it open for me.

I took my time standing up and walking across the room. "Thank you." I stepped inside and listened to the door close behind me.

Her office wasn't what I was expecting. It wasn't elegant and feminine the way Titan's was. A large olive green desk sat near the back wall, which was entirely made of glass. Her office was unusual because it jutted out farther than the rest, so every single wall was nothing but windows. Two large tables were along the other walls, covered with note-books with scribbled notes and calculators. There were electrical apparatuses as well, things I couldn't even identify.

Two lone chairs faced her desk.

Ms. Alexander rose from her seat wearing a skintight black dress with a deep blue cardigan on top. She greeted me with a smile, but it certainly wasn't genuine. "Nice to see you again, Mr. Cutler."

I stopped at her desk and shook her hand. "You as well." The second my hand latched on to hers, the same erotic images flashed across my mind. I had her in my bed, her thighs squeezing my waist as her dress was pushed to her stomach. Her panties were still hanging off one ankle because she was too desperate for me to take the time to remove them. Her nails dug into my ass, and she pulled me deep into her because she wanted me to fuck her even harder.

Goddamn.

I quickly pulled my hand away then unbuttoned my suit coat before I sat down.

Shake it off. "Thank you for meeting with me."

"My pleasure." She straightened her dress before she sat down.

I wanted to show her the real meaning of pleasure.

She held herself straight, her posture perfect and her gaze poised. "You've reconsidered our business arrangement?"

"I have." I sat erect in the chair, my powerful shoulders covering the chair from her view. My knees were spread, and my feet were firmly planted against the floor. My arms rested on the armrests, and I stared her down with my intimidating gaze. People were usually unnerved by me. I could keep a conversation going even in silence. I was the strong and silent type, especially with women. Titan was the only woman I actually spoke to. No reason to talk when you were fucking.

Ms. Alexander waited for me to say something, and when nothing happened for thirty seconds, she spoke again. "And?"

She wore a different shade of lipstick that day, and it was hard not to stare at it. She wore a different necklace too. Her watch was still the same, the pristine rose gold color. She had beautiful skin and a slender neck. My teeth wanted to drag across the skin, just to feel how delicate she really was. Something about her power made me more aggressive. I wanted to snuff out of her presence, to overrule her in every way possible. I respected her strength, but that also wanted to make me break her even more. "I should have been more transparent in that meeting."

She tilted her head slightly, showing her confusion but never dropping her confidence. "I think you were perfectly clear, Mr. Cutler. You aren't looking for a partnership, and I am. No confusion." She sounded sexy while sounding professional at the same time. I wasn't sure how she accomplished it.

"I think if I'd been clearer you would have changed your mind."

Her mood noticeably darkened to the color of

her hair. "No. I'm not the kind of woman who changes her mind."

"Five billion." It was more than what I wrote on the paper in my office, but I wanted to offer something she couldn't resist. Maybe her company was worth hundreds of millions, but she wasn't even close to her first billion. Any person would flinch at that kind of money.

But she didn't. "Alexander Applications isn't for sale, Mr. Cutler."

"Ten billion."

She didn't even blink. "You're wasting your time."

I'd just put a ridiculous offer on the table, and she didn't even nibble. Now I knew this woman had never been playing a game with me. She was more straightforward than I realized. She said exactly what she meant. "Give me a number, Ms. Alexander."

"Money may mean everything to you, but it means nothing to me. You can go now." As if the meeting was over, she grabbed her blank tablet and unlocked the screen. "Give my best to Titan. I hope she recovers soon."

I stayed in my seat, refusing to leave until I got what I wanted. There was no other trick up my sleeve. I didn't know how to bargain with someone when money wasn't a chip I could use. She wanted a vision; she wanted a future. "Help me understand, Ms. Alexander. Help me understand how a business-woman could reject the greatest offer she'll ever receive."

She finished what she was doing on her tablet before she set it down again. "For such an intelligent man, you seem to absorb information very slowly. I told you money doesn't mean anything to me. I'm basically telling you I'm a vegetarian, but you continue to offer me prime rib. Offer me something I want, and maybe we can move forward." She looked at me again, her green eyes hypnotic. I could feel her soft skin just by looking at it. My fingers ached to explore that shiny hair.

"Money means something to everyone. Let's not pretend you're different from the rest of us."

"It does," she said simply. "But after you reach a certain point, it doesn't matter. My life isn't any different whether I have one hundred million dollars or one billion. It's exactly the same."

"If that were true, you wouldn't want to work with Titan. You know she'll elevate your standing considerably."

"She will," she said. "But she'll also bring my technology to a new level as well. If I simply sell, she'll have the authority to do whatever she wants. While I respect Ms. Titan, I don't know her. I've never met the woman. How can I trust her to do the right thing with this power? I can't. I need to be there —as her partner. Just as Einstein built the technology for the atomic bomb, it was used for evil. I need to make sure my inventions are used appropriately."

"Titan operates on a strict code of ethics. You don't need to worry about her."

"I'm sure you're right. But I sleep better at night knowing I have equal say. I believe a partnership will allow me to grow as an entrepreneur and explore different areas of business. I also believe it will allow me to grow as a person, to give me the kind of legacy that people will remember long after I'm gone. Titan is a respectable woman with a brilliant mind. I want to be viewed in the same way."

"So this is about fame?"

She considered my question long before she answered. "No. It's about respect."

Titan cared about her image immensely. It took her a long time to earn the respect of the world, to be treated equally. It was a heavy burden on her shoulders, and sometimes the weight was too heavy. But she never let it defeat her. It made her stand stronger, made her prouder. Even though she could give up everything and hide away as a very wealthy woman, she loved it too much. She loved being a role model, a symbol for women everywhere.

Ms. Alexander was exactly the same.

It really wasn't about money.

"Titan isn't interested in a partnership. I've already said that."

"Yes." She kept her shoulders back and her chest forward, and her firm tits were difficult not to stare at. Even if I didn't look at them, everything about her was innately sexy. Her slender shoulders led to small arms. She had a hint of a bicep, and her forearms were defined. The diamond earrings in her lobes reflected the light coming in from the windows. Her face was her most beautiful feature. With almond-shaped eyes, a small nose, and a few freckles on her cheeks, she was absolutely lovely. Her full lips were the most distracting. They were so plump and thick. God, they would feel wonderful against my mouth.

Thorn, stop.

I tried to stop thinking about her looks and focus on the conversation. "I've known Titan for a long time, and I know her better than almost anyone." Diesel had replaced me. "She's not going to change her mind. I suggest you reconsider. I'm not saying this to get what I want. But I think you're losing a great opportunity here."

"I'm sure you're being sincere," she said casually. "But again, I'm simply not interested in that route."

Now that there was nothing more to say, I held her gaze. I could do it for hours, just stare at her sparkling green eyes and her fair cheeks. Her dark hair made her skin appear even lighter, even though it had a nice rosy color to it. Her mouth was just as hypnotizing as her eyes. As if someone had constructed her to portray the overwhelming beauty of a painting, she was stunning. The more I looked at her, the more I couldn't deny it. "I saw you went to MIT. That's impressive." I was a very busy man, so I wasn't much of a conversationalist. I didn't care to learn more about my potential business partners. All I wanted to know was what they had to offer. But the comment came out of my mouth all on its own.

"And I also dropped out of MIT."

For some reason, that impressed me even more. She got into one of the most esteemed colleges in the world, but even that wasn't good enough for her. "How long were you there?"

"One semester."

"What made you leave?"

"My ideas. My studies were too time-consuming

and distracting. All I wanted to do was work on a solar cell model, so I decided to take a permanent hiatus to focus on my passions. A lot of people said it was a stupid idea, and I enjoyed proving them wrong."

Just by the limited conversation between us, I could tell this woman's intelligence exceeded mine —by a landslide. I had strength in business, but she had strength in a discipline I couldn't even pretend to understand. Not only was she a remarkable scientist, but she managed to create a product that made a lot of money. Titan was right when she warned me not to underestimate this woman.

"You went to Yale, right?"

My eyebrows rose when I realized she'd read up on me. "Yes."

"That's a great school."

"It's no MIT."

"School is supposed to prepare you for the real world, but honestly, the only thing that can prepare you for the real world is yourself."

I didn't ask her for an elaboration because I knew she was speaking from her personal life. When I researched her, I found a lot of detailed specifics about her work but not much about her.

Her technology took all the fame, but very few people knew she was the one behind it.

I found myself wanting to stay and continue this conversation, but I knew it was both pointless and inappropriate. I would have to disappoint Titan and say the deal wasn't going to happen. And I would have to walk away from this woman and forget about her. A part of me wanted to ask her to get a drink with me, but I knew it would be a conflict of interest. Besides, she didn't strike me as the kind of woman who'd be interested in casual sex. I wasn't even sure if she was attracted to me. It was difficult to read that hard mask of hers. She was professional to the point of making Titan seem amateur. "Thank you for your time. I wish you the best for Alexander Applications." I rose to my feet.

Her eyes immediately glanced down, looking right at my crotch. She held the look for a few heartbeats before she met my gaze again.

I glanced down to button the front of my jacket, and that's when I noticed the huge bulge in the front of my slacks. I was used to having a hard-on anytime I was around this woman, so I didn't even notice. My fingers pushed the button through the hole, and I looked at her again, not feeling any shame for the big dick in my pants.

I didn't care if she knew I wanted to fuck her.

My jacket covered most of the bulge, but it was obviously still there.

She glanced at it again, this time, her gaze piercing. "You too. I know there are very *big* things in your future."

Maybe she was attracted to me, after all.

"Goodbye, Ms. Alexander." I turned around without shaking her hand since I had already exchanged something much more personal with her. I walked to the door and didn't wait for her to return the greeting.

And she never did.

TITAN GREETED ME WITH A WIDE SMILE AND WRAPPED her arms around me. She hugged me for a while, standing on her own two feet inside her penthouse. It was the first hug we'd shared since before she was shot. She'd been too injured for an embrace, and I was afraid I would give her an infection.

But now I finally hugged her.

I held her small frame against me and sighed in relief. It was a gift to see her on her feet, even if she was moving slower than she usually did. That smile lit up my entire life. Knowing she was happy made me happy. "You look great."

"Thanks." She pulled away, her eyes still lit up. "I feel a lot better. Still taking things slow and not working, but it's nice not to be in the hospital anymore."

"I can tell. You're like a new woman."

"Well, I also got laid last night," she said with a chuckle. "That did wonders too..."

I chuckled before I winked at her. "It's a cure for almost anything."

Diesel walked up to me next and shook my hand. "Nice to see you, man."

"You too." Now I felt like an idiot for not believing Diesel when he said he was telling the truth. Because of my miscalculation, Titan had almost died. I said a lot of cold and cruel things to him, but he somehow forgave me for all of it. A part of me would always feel guilty, especially when I saw him taking care of her now. "You're a male gigolo now?"

"You could say that," he said with a laugh. "I feel like that's all she wants from me most of the time, especially since she doesn't eat."

Titan rolled her eyes. "I eat."

"Sorry, I'm on his side for this one, Titan," I said. "You never eat."

"But you're right." Titan rose on her tiptoes and kissed him on the mouth. "That is all I want from you."

He smiled against her mouth and pulled her tighter into his body. He was shirtless and in just his sweatpants, and he didn't think twice before pulling her close and intensifying their affection.

I walked around them and made myself a drink at the bar. I could hear the kissing noises they made, but at least I didn't have to look at them.

They finally broke apart when I sat on the couch. Titan sat beside me, taking her time getting into the cushion. She wore a t-shirt, and the gauze was visible through the fabric. She winced slightly when she moved, but she didn't seem to be in overwhelming pain.

"How's the pain?" I asked.

"It gets better every day," she said. "I can sleep through the night now."

"That's great."

"So, did you acquire that deal with Ms. Alexander?" She switched back into business mode, like her wound couldn't slow her down. Her mind was still on business no matter what her health issues were.

I shook my head slightly. "I tried."

"What do you mean?" she asked. "That's an expression I don't understand."

I smirked because I knew she was being serious. "I went to her office, which I wasn't happy about, and I talked to her again. I made the offer, and she didn't blink. I doubled it, and she still didn't blink. Titan... she's not like the rest. This woman is different. She's not after money."

"Then what is she after?"

"Legacy." It was something Titan understood all too well. "She wants to be recognized for her work. She wants to be a female powerhouse. She wants to change the world. And she either wants to do it with you or on her own...but she won't sell her work to anyone."

Titan's eyes shifted back and forth as she looked into mine.

"She's smart, Titan. One of the smartest people I've ever spoken to. Her brainwaves are on a different planet entirely. I know you don't partner with anyone, but you're going to have to make an exception this time. Because being her competitor isn't going to be easy either. She's got the skills to match you."

"You speak highly of her."

How could I not? "She earned my respect."

A slow smile stretched across her lips. "I think she earned something else too."

Diesel chuckled as he sat on the other couch. "You got it hard for this woman."

"I'm attracted to her." I didn't deny it. "But that's it."

"And there's no possibility of changing her mind?" Titan asked.

I shook my head. "No. Not possible."

Titan leaned back against the couch and crossed her legs. "Maybe I should meet her in person…"

"It'll have to wait a few weeks until you're back on your feet," Diesel said.

"I am back on my feet," Titan countered.

Diesel gave her a hard look. "You know what I mean, baby. If you wanna have this argument in front of Thorn, fine. But you know I'm going to win."

Titan rolled her eyes.

"I'm on his side for this one too," I said. "You were shot, Titan. You shouldn't be working. I can handle it."

"But I can handle Ms. Alexander," she countered.

I shook my head. "Not even you could get her, Titan. Trust me when I say that. Diesel couldn't make a dent in her armor either. Money won't work with her. It doesn't mean anything to her."

"Money means something to everyone," Titan said. "You're lying if you say otherwise."

"It does mean something to her," I said. "But not as much as it means to us. She won't sell. She'll only partner. If I thought there were the possibility of making it work, I would tell you. But there's not. She's more stubborn than all three of us combined. So you're going to have to consider her request if you really want to work with her."

Titan considered what I said in silence before she turned to Diesel. "What do you think?"

"You've never asked me that before." He drank his scotch before he set it on the table.

"We're going to spend our lives together. My success is your success. So I'm going to be asking you that a lot more often." Titan stared at Diesel with that commanding gaze, stealing his entire focus with just her expression.

He stared at her like I wasn't even there. Slowly, a smile stretched across his face. "I like that."

"Then what do you think?" she asked.

Diesel turned his gaze back on me. "If Thorn is

right about this woman, then you don't have a choice. You can either work with her and monopolize the market with someone who's obviously a genius, or you can compete against her. You may have cash and the experience to market your company, but you can't compete with her technology. She'll always find a way to improve current products, to make them better and more affordable. So you'll always be trailing behind her, constantly playing catch-up. I know you don't like it when other people have more power over you, but that's the situation. Alexander has the edge this time."

Diesel put it nicely, and I couldn't have agreed more. "So, what do you want to do, Titan?"

"I need to think about it for a little bit," Titan said. "Sleep on it."

At least she didn't reject the idea altogether. Titan was already invested in solar energy, and she would lose a lot more money walking away from it than acquiring a partner. I grabbed my drink and sipped it as I sat back. "Everything else at your offices is going well. Nothing out of the ordinary."

"That's good to hear," Titan said. "Thanks so much for helping me, Thorn."

"You're welcome, Titan."

8

TITAN

I LAID out his suit and tie and made him a cup of coffee to-go.

Diesel walked out of the bathroom with a towel wrapped around his waist. Water drops still clung to his powerful shoulders. When his body was chiseled and wet, it was nearly irresistible. I wanted to drag my tongue along the grooves and lick all the drops away. He stopped when he saw his clothes laid out on the bed. "Baby, what are you up to?" He pulled the towel from around his waist and tossed it in the laundry basket.

I'd seen him naked hundreds of times, but I was never prepared for how delicious he looked. All hard muscle, masculine curves, and strong lines. He was absolutely beautiful, drop-dead gorgeous.

"Baby?" He grinned, knowing exactly why I hadn't said anything yet.

I snapped myself out of it. "You're going to work today."

His smile immediately dropped as he walked toward me. "I'm not going anywhere."

"Diesel, I'm fine. I never took you as a man to ignore all of his responsibilities because of something like this. Life goes on."

"You're right, and normally, I wouldn't. But the second you put on that ring, you became the most important thing in my life." His hand moved to my cheek, his long fingers reaching my hair. "Work is important, but it'll never be more important than you."

Just like every other time he touched me, I melted right on the spot. I forgot my point because he erased all my thoughts with his handsome gaze. "I know. But I'm fine, Diesel. I don't need you to stay here with me all day."

"I'm not leaving you." He pulled his hand away and grabbed the suit off the bed. He returned it to the hanger and placed the navy blue suit back in the closet. "The second you're back to normal, I'll put a suit on—but not to go to work." He came back to me, still naked and scorching.

"Then why would you put one on?"

His arms circled my waist, and he rubbed his nose against mine. "So I can marry you."

THE BUZZER FROM THE ELEVATOR SOUNDED.

Diesel left the couch, shirtless in his sweatpants, and answered it. "Who's there?" Even though Bruce Carol was gone, Diesel had become a million times more protective. He didn't beat around the bush. He was suspicious—and he didn't hide it.

"Your father," Vincent said over the speaker. "Thought I could stop by."

"Come up." Diesel hit the button so the elevator would open. "Is it alright if my dad stops by?"

"Of course. I'd love to see him."

Diesel walked into the bedroom and pulled on a shirt before he came back out.

The elevator doors opened at the same time, and Vincent walked inside. He carried a clear vase of flowers, an arrangement of purple, blue, and white flowers.

"Are those for me?" I met him by the door and immediately took the vase from his hands.

He smiled. "Diesel told me you liked flowers."

Diesel snatched the vase from me before I could even carry the weight. "Did he also tell you that Titan isn't allowed to carry anything?"

"Diesel," I said. "I can carry—"

"No." Like the conversation was over, he walked to one of the couch tables and set the vase down.

Vincent slid his hands into his pockets and shrugged. "I'm glad you like them, Titan. He told me lilies are your favorite, but I thought I'd let him be the one to get those for you."

"Thank you, Vincent." I hugged him, feeling his beefy size in my arms. It was like hugging Diesel, another brick wall. "Can I get you anything?"

"I'll get it." Diesel still carried his brooding attitude, interfering with everything I tried to do. "Dad, what do you want?"

"Water is fine." He walked with me to the couches in the living room. Diesel was in the kitchen, out of earshot. "Has he driven you crazy yet?"

"A long time ago," I said with a laugh. "But he means well, so I let it slide."

"Yeah." He sat on the other couch, his arms resting on his knees. "He does mean well. In fact, I've never seen him be more attentive in my life."

Diesel walked out a moment later and handed him the glass.

Vincent took a drink before he set it on the table. "Thank you, son."

Diesel sat beside me on the couch, his arm resting over the back of the couch while his other hand rested on my arm. His fingers gently brushed against me, and he didn't seem to care about our PDA in front of his father.

"How are you?" Vincent only looked at me, removing Diesel from the conversation.

"I feel great. Things are getting better every day."

"That's good," Vincent said. "You seem happier."

I was happy now that I was getting sex again, but I wasn't going to say that to him. "I am."

"I know Thorn is handling your affairs right now, but I know we talked about us working together with Kyle. I was wondering if you wanted to get that going. All we need to do is get everything with the distributors and we're good."

"She's not working right now, Dad," Diesel threatened. "I already said that."

He raised his hand. "I apologize. I was just going to ask if it was okay if I talked to Thorn about this."

Diesel turned into the protective bear that he'd become. "She's not—"

"Yes, you can pass that along to Thorn," I said. "I think it's a great idea, and he'll handle it."

"Alright," Vincent said. "That's all I wanted to know."

Diesel released a heavy sigh that came off as a growl.

Vincent ignored it like he didn't hear it. "I'm going to the Founder's Charity on Saturday night. Will you be attending, Diesel?"

"No." He didn't provide a detailed explanation. If I wasn't there beside him, then he obviously didn't see the point. The only place he wanted to be was home with me. "I'm sure Thorn is going, though."

Vincent nodded. "I'll see him there, then."

"Are you taking anyone?" I asked, wondering if he was still seeing that woman.

Vincent rubbed his palms together. "I'm going alone. I broke it off with that woman I was seeing... just didn't work out."

I wondered if that meant he took my words to heart, that he might try to find something more serious rather than young companions. "Are you alright?"

"I'm fine," Vincent said. "It was never serious."

Diesel didn't ask him any questions about it. It must be awkward for him to listen to it.

"Is there anything I can get you?" Vincent asked. "Some groceries?"

"No thanks," Diesel answered. "I have one of my guys get it."

Vincent leaned back into the couch then glanced at the TV. He wore an expensive black watch, a midnight color that matched his constant shadow. He was formidable without even trying to be. His silent hostility was similar to Diesel's. Even at the happiest of times, they were brooding. "This must be hard for you, Titan. I know you aren't the kind of woman who enjoys sitting around."

"It's been hell," I said with a sigh. "All I do is sit around and eat."

"Which is exactly what you should be doing," Diesel said coldly.

"How long will you be recovering for?" Vincent asked.

"Maybe another week—"

"At least a month," Diesel answered.

I'd go crazy if I were cooped up in this place for an entire month. I'd lose my mind. "Uh, I don't think so."

"Until the doctor removes that gauze and clears you, you aren't going anywhere." Diesel didn't look at me as he said it, staring forward at the TV. "That's the end of the discussion."

I rolled my eyes. "Stop saying it's the end of the discussion. You know it's never the end when it comes to me."

Diesel didn't rise to the humor. "She won't be back at work for at least a month." He repeated what he'd already said, as if he were carving it into stone.

"Then you need to go back to work," I said. "You can't stay here with me for another month. You have a lot to take care of."

"I agree with her," Vincent said. "Staying home with her has been the right thing to do, but you can't do it forever. You have an empire to manage, and you need to check on hers as well. Even if your businesses seem to be thriving without your presence, you can't trust all the people below you. Some will remain loyal, but most won't. The second you turn your back, they'll serve their best interests. She has Thorn, but you don't have anyone."

Diesel didn't say anything, his jaw tensing slightly.

I turned to him, seeing the conflict in his eyes. "Go back to work, Diesel."

"We'll talk about it later," he said quietly.

I knew he didn't want to leave me even though I

was getting around the house well. I could take my medication on my own and shower just fine. My independence was returning, and the pain was starting to dip even further. If I really needed something, he was just a phone call away.

Vincent hung around for thirty minutes before he left. He gave me a hug by the door and a kiss on the cheek before he disappeared into the elevator. I knew he'd come to see me, not as an excuse to see his son. I felt like I had my own relationship with Diesel's father, and he'd become more than just a father-in-law to me. He reminded me of my own father in a lot of ways.

He looked at me the way my father used to.

Diesel turned to me when we were alone again. "I'll stay with you for another week. And then we'll see how you feel before we decide if I should return to the office."

"Diesel, I'm fine right now. Go back."

He stared at me with the same reluctance in his eyes. The longer he stayed with me, the more work piled up. But his devotion to me outweighed all the stress waiting for him at the office.

"Why don't you go to work in the morning and come back every day for a long lunch?" I asked. "That way, you can check on me. After that, you can go back to work until the end of the day, then come home. Honestly, I just sit around all day and do nothing. If I'm going crazy, then you must be losing your mind too."

"I'm happy to be with you, baby." He stared into my eyes with overwhelming sincerity. He never lied to me, so everything he said meant so much. There was always a layer of affection on the surface of his eyes, a look reserved only for me. He may have bedded hundreds of women before, some two at a time, but it felt like there'd never been anyone before me. I was the only thing that actually mattered to him. "The only reason I want to go back is because my father's right. My presence is important. It keeps people in line."

"I couldn't agree more."

"Thorn is doing you a huge favor, but I don't have anyone who can do that for me."

"He would do it for you too, if you asked."

He shook his head slightly. "No offense to him, but I wouldn't want him to. The only person I would trust is my father...but he's busier than I am."

I couldn't stop the smile from stretching across my face. Their relationship took a while to rebuild, but with every passing day, it became stronger. I saw their connection deepen once tragedy struck.

Vincent was there for me because he cared about me, but he was also there for his son.

Diesel smiled before he released a sigh. "Don't look at me like that."

"What? I like to smile."

"But I know why you're smiling."

"You do?" I moved into his chest and rose on my tiptoes. My hands pressed against his strong frame for balance, and I leaned in and kissed him.

He kissed me back, his strong arms wrapping tightly around my waist. His embrace was sensual and slow, but it held all of his longing and passion for me. His fingers gripped my body, but his pressure was full of restraint. He didn't handle me as aggressively as he used to, purposely being gentle with me even when he didn't want to. He used to grab the back of my hair and jerk my head into position so he could kiss me. Sometimes he would take me by the back of the neck and bend me over the bed when I least expected it. Then he would fuck me as hard as he wanted without warning.

But now, only a gentle giant remained.

When he pulled away, he looked me in the eye, his love obvious. "I'll think it over for a while."

My fingers slipped underneath his t-shirt and up his muscular stomach. I felt the hard abs and the rivers in between as I moved to his chest. When I touched the flat slab of defined flesh, my fingers pressed into him even harder. He was warm, hard, and bursting with constant testosterone. "While you're thinking about that, you want to please your woman?"

The corner of his lips rose in a smile. "My woman doesn't have to ask to be pleased."

9

THORN

MY DREAM JOLTED ME AWAKE.

It was white-hot, sweaty, and sexy as hell. I didn't want the vision to leave my gaze, but the jolt of pleasure sparked my body into consciousness. I sat up in bed and looked into the darkness of my bedroom. Light was shining through my blackout shutters, which told me morning had arrived.

My chest was covered in sweat, and my dick was harder than a solid slab of stone.

The vision of Ms. Alexander slowly faded away. She was on her knees in front of me, trying to suck my enormous dick with that big mouth of hers. Spit drooled from the corners of her lips, and tears fell from the corners of her eyes. She wanted to suck more of my dick, but her slender throat was simply too small.

But that didn't stop her from trying.

I ran my fingers through my hair then rubbed the sleep from the inside edge of my eye. My clock showed the time, and I only had two minutes before my alarm went off. It'd been a long while since my last fling. The drama with Titan had put my personal life on hold, and after she was shot, I hadn't been interested in sex.

But Ms. Alexander awakened me again.

I spat on my palm then wrapped my fingers around my cock. I closed my eyes and recreated the dream in my head.

Then I jerked off, pretending my hand was Ms. Alexander's tight lips.

I HAD A SUIT MADE BY CONNOR SUEDE, JET BLACK with a matching tie. It fit me to a T, with crisp fabric and a cut that molded to my musculature perfectly. Fashion wasn't important to me, but suits were a different story.

I cared about my suits.

They projected my power and wealth. They projected my darkness, my constant hostility. For a man of my stature, I had to convey my confidence. I was in a sea of suits everywhere I went. I had to stand out.

My driver took me to the Founder's Charity event at the Plaza. I was dateless because I was always dateless—with the exception of Titan. I'd be ignorant to think people forgot about my relationship with her in light of the shooting. She may have spun the tale to make it sound like a beautiful love story, but I still got the short straw.

I was still the one who got dumped.

The women who'd actually fucked me knew I was a catch. More times than not, they told me they wanted something more. They wanted to stay that way forever—and that's when I cut them loose. Not only was I great in bed, but I was a bit of a gentleman. I treated women with respect. Titan could vouch for that.

But now the world saw me through different eyes.

Like I gave a damn.

My friendship with Titan meant more to me than the opinion of the entire world. With her, I had something irreplaceable. I had a level of trust I didn't share with anyone else. We would never have the same last name and we would never make a family together, but she was more of my family than my own parents.

I loved her.

I didn't care if that made me sound like a pussy.

I arrived at the hotel and entered the ballroom with one hand in my pocket. Socializing with the elites of Manhattan was easy and necessary. Business opportunities presented themselves at the most unsuspecting moments. Being well connected was just as important as putting in an eight-hour workday. I could have easily skipped the event, but I knew it was essential to keep up relationships.

I mingled for a while, and almost everyone asked how Titan was doing. Their perception of me was a little different, I could feel it. But the more we talked, the more normal it seemed. If I retained my same level of confidence, people would only focus on that —not my relationship with Titan.

Eventually, everyone would forget about it.

But that would take a while.

I saw a familiar face as I finished my champagne. I set the empty flute on a passing tray and walked up to Vincent Hunt, a large man who wore his suit better than a mannequin. He didn't have a beautiful woman on his arm like he usually did. Tonight, he was alone. "How's it going?"

He shook my hand, breaking his stern expression and giving me a welcoming smile. "Good. How are you?"

"Just making an appearance. I get sick of these bullshit functions."

His grin widened. "At least you're honest enough to admit it."

"No date this evening?"

He placed both hands in his pockets. "I'm not seeing anyone right now."

The last woman I saw him with was exceptional. I was surprised he let her go. But then again, I had a quick turnaround rate too. In fact, mine was faster than his. At least he stayed with the same woman for a few months. I was gone after a few weeks. "That's too bad."

He barely shrugged. "What about you?"

"My life has been too hectic lately..." I couldn't remember the last time I even went to a bar for a drink. My life had been going nonstop. It was nightmare after nightmare. I missed my old life, when everything was going my way.

"I saw Titan yesterday." A man he knew passed, and he gave him a nod in acknowledgment but didn't try to speak to him. "She looks better every time I see her. Just a little restless."

"Sitting at home all day is driving her crazy. No doubt about that."

"You're a good friend for looking after her affairs. Not too many people would do that." Vincent stared at me with his deep look, his brown eyes looking like dark lasers. He was a man with a staring problem, but he didn't bother correcting it. It was a useful tool for him, to have more confidence than most of his acquaintances.

"She'd do the same for me." I didn't think twice when it came to Titan. If she needed me, I was there. We'd formed a blood oath long before I'd killed Jeremy. We were bound together by something that defied the laws of physics. No matter what, I always had her back. She had mine.

"I'm sure she would. That's still generous of you. You have your own business to worry about."

My business was different than hers. I was born into a wealthy family, descended from generations that revolved around this company. My great-grandfather started it when he was young, and now it belonged to me. Unlike Titan, I didn't truly work for it. It was the reason I started a few other companies, that way I'd have a different legacy to give my children. "Her best interests are my best interests."

"I'm sure letting her go was hard. You're a good man for stepping aside."

"I didn't lose her." She was never mine in the way she belonged to Diesel. Our relationship hadn't changed at all. It was only based on friendship and convenience. I found her attractive, but I didn't get hard for her the way I did with other women...like Ms. Alexander. "She's exactly what she's always been to me—my friend."

"Even so, I'm sure you were looking forward to having her as your wife."

My situation definitely would have been simpler. I'd never find anyone better to share my life. Titan was so easy to get along with. And she accepted me for exactly who I was. Most women weren't like that. That was what I wanted in a partner—someone who accepted me. I was a hard worker, and I was fiercely loyal. I was always honest. But I was incapable of feeling romantic love. Everything else was there, so that was the only piece that was missing. All women wanted more, wanting a happily ever after. Titan was the only one who didn't—until she met Diesel. "It definitely made my life easier. But I'm happy for her. I feel like an idiot for not believing Diesel in the first place. It was stupid."

"He doesn't hold a grudge."

"Doesn't matter." I still felt like shit about it. Titan had been shot because of it. "Diesel is a great guy. Since he loves Titan, he'll be a part of my family. He's a powerful man with a lot of connections. I don't mind having him in my inner circle."

"Who else is in your inner circle?"

"Just Titan." I was close to my parents, and honestly, I was a bit of a mama's boy. But they didn't make the cut because I couldn't be completely honest with them. I had my friends I went out with, but they didn't count either. Only Titan had earned my unflinching trust. I could tell her I killed someone, and she'd help me hide the body—no judgments.

Vincent gave a slight nod. "I don't have anyone in my inner circle. You're lucky you have someone."

"What about Jax?"

"I'm close to him, but I can never have a son in that circle. I have to be a role model to them. My skeletons need to remain hidden away."

"You don't seem like a man who has skeletons."

He nodded to a woman who walked by, a pretty lady who flashed him a smile. He turned back to me. "Everyone has skeletons, Thorn. If you don't, you aren't that interesting."

That was true. "I'm glad you and Diesel are

getting along. Your fight was getting bloody." I looked past his shoulder as my eyes settled on a curvy woman with dark hair. It was in open curls, luscious and shiny. In a skintight black dress that showed her flat stomach and tight ass, the woman was beautiful from head to toe. My gaze turned back to Vincent, only because I forced it to.

"I'm grateful to move on. I became a different person in my rage. I got carried away…"

My eyes shifted back toward the woman as she turned around. She was speaking to a man in a suit, but I didn't pay attention to his face. All I cared about was her. With bright green eyes, a few freckles on her cheeks, and plump lips, she was the center of attention for the entire room. Most of the men were looking at her.

Ms. Alexander.

I hadn't expected her to be there that night. Once I realized it was her, my cock hardened in my slacks automatically. Like she was the only woman in the world who had control over it, she could manipulate it with just a smile. My slacks suddenly tightened in front as my gaze took her the swell of her tits and the curve of her hips. "We all get carried away from time to time…"

I FINISHED MY GLASS OF SCOTCH BEFORE I MOVED IN.

I approached her from the left, just as she finished her conversation with one of the Rocker brothers. It would be easy for me to ignore her since there was nothing to say, but my cock certainly couldn't stop thinking about her.

And the way she stared at my crotch.

It would be one thing if she'd simply glanced at him, but her stare lasted for several seconds. A new blush entered her cheeks, and her eyes intensified in eagerness. I wasn't ashamed of the monster cock outlined in my slacks, and she obviously wasn't ashamed to look at him either.

Sexy.

I didn't think anything would ever happen with this woman, but that didn't stop me from walking up to her. She was smarter than the women I usually bedded, blazing with obvious self-respect. She could have any man she wanted, and she was probably looking for a renowned intellectual who would settle down with her. She could demand a commitment out of anyone and get it in a second.

But that wasn't me.

She must have felt me staring at her because

her gaze shifted in my direction. She must have seen me earlier because she didn't seem remotely surprised by my presence. Or she was just exceptionally good at wearing a poker face. She held a glass flute of bubbling champagne, and a slight smile formed on her lips at the sight of me. She could be so sexy without even trying. If her scientist gig didn't work out, she could be a model if she wanted.

I stopped in front of her, my hands resting in my pockets. I didn't shake her hand because it didn't feel right.

We were beyond shaking hands.

Now that I was face-to-face with her, seeing those thick eyelashes and sexy eye makeup, I didn't have anything to say. Staring at her was enough entertainment for me. I didn't know if it was her rigid backbone or the elegant posture, but something stole my entire focus. I'd never been around a woman more certain of herself. Most of the people in this room were male business tycoons with their trophy wives, but she didn't seem even slightly intimidated. Her strength was sexy, her confidence hypnotizing.

She was one hell of a woman.

A minute had passed, but I didn't speak. My eyes

remained glued to hers, the intensity only increasing.

She didn't stiffen at my penetrating gaze. She didn't break eye contact or even blink. She stayed strong, not bowing to anyone.

Not bowing to me.

She refused to speak first, and I knew it was because she wanted to maintain the power in the situation.

I'd gladly give it to her. "Are you having a good time?" I wanted to say she looked beautiful, but a gorgeous woman like her didn't need to hear the compliment—for the hundredth time that night. She noticed every single stare that came her way. She knew she was the object of a lot of men's fantasies. She was too much of a genius not to pick up on it. So she didn't need to hear me say it. All she had to do was look down—and she would know how I felt about her.

"Good champagne and good company." She took a sip then licked her lips.

I watched her tongue swipe across her bottom lip, and I immediately thought about that sweet mouth around my cock. I'd jerked off to her early that morning, and I felt like doing it again. Or better yet, getting the real thing. "Are you here with anyone?" I'd never considered it before, but she was probably seeing someone. A woman like her couldn't stay single long.

"No."

It was a good answer, but it didn't answer the question I really wanted to know.

"How's Titan doing?"

"Well. She'll be at home for another month before she comes back to the office." Whether she actually cared or not, I appreciated the question.

"It's nice of you to take over her companies... considering you aren't together anymore."

Whenever I talked to her, I forgot about the fallacy that surrounded me. Like everyone else, Ms. Alexander thought I had been engaged to Titan because I loved her—and she'd left me for someone else. But when it was just the two of us, it didn't seem like anything else really mattered. "Together or apart, I'll always be there for her."

Her eyes softened for the very first time.

I didn't want to talk about Titan anymore, not when I was lying about my feelings for her. "Have you had a change of heart about what we discussed?"

"No. You?"

"Titan is considering it."

"She is?" Her voice picked up slightly, filled with an obvious sense of hope.

"I told her you weren't going to change your mind under any circumstance."

"I'm glad you finally understand me."

The corner of my mouth rose in a smile. "Took me long enough, huh?"

She smiled back, and that simple reaction made my cock stir in my slacks.

Why did this woman get me so hard?

"I sincerely hope Titan changes her mind. I would love the opportunity to work with her. I really mean it when I say I think we could do great things together."

The more I interacted with her, the more I agreed with her. Ms. Alexander had a special quality that would make her an invaluable member of Titan's staff. I could see her intelligence every time I looked at her. She reminded me of Titan in many ways, just a different version of her. "I'll put in a good word for you."

"Yeah?" Her smile widened. "You don't know me very well, Mr. Cutler."

"Then let me get to know you better." I moved a little closer to her, almost crossing the line and invading her personal space entirely. If she didn't want me this close to her, she would have just told me. But she held my gaze, her eyes playful. This was the time I would spit out a line or cut right to the chase. But I didn't do any of those things. I respected her too much, and respect was hard to earn from me. I wanted her if she wanted me, and now I was waiting for her invitation. I wanted to slide my hand into her hair and kiss those plump lips, but I kept my hands to myself. Being in control was something I did best. I wanted to tell her exactly what I wanted— and watch her obey.

But that wouldn't work on a woman like her.

She spoke with a sexy voice, deep and sultry. "What do you want to know?"

I wanted to know if her lips tasted like champagne. I wanted to know how my name sounded on her tongue. I wanted to know if she slept alone at night or if there was a man beside her. I wanted to know if she wanted me to please her, to give her my big dick that she was so fond of. I wanted to know if she wanted me the way I wanted her. I wanted to know how she would feel if she knew I'd jerked off to her that morning.

But I also wanted to know other things.

I wanted to know where her passion came from. I wanted to know what her favorite drink was. I wanted to know if she listened to music while she was in her lab. If so, what did she enjoy? I wanted to know if she preferred the pandemonium of the city, or if she had a place across the bridge. I wanted to know what her hopes and dreams were. "Anything you want to share with me."

"First round is on me." I stood beside her at the bar and clanked my glass against hers. I had a scotch on the rocks with a twist. She had a glass of red wine. I wasn't a fan of wine. I preferred liquor or beer, regardless of what I was eating.

"Thank you." She kept her eyes on me as she took a drink. She peered at me from under her thick eyelashes. Her green eyes sparkled even more with the dim lighting in the bar. There were people everywhere, but we had a nice spot in the corner. The loud chatter overhead only gave me an excuse to get closer to her. Sometimes my arm brushed against hers when I moved. If I moved my leg a little more, I could touch hers.

But I didn't.

At this angle, I could get a nice view down the top of her dress. She had small tits, but they were perky as hell. Whenever she looked away, I could easily enjoy the sight with my perverted gaze.

But I never looked.

I never pretended to be something I wasn't. I was honest with my intentions, and I was always honest about who I was inside. I was the kind of man who used women to please myself. They got pleasure out of it too, but that didn't make it meaningful. With anyone else, I probably would look down her dress.

But I didn't do it to Ms. Alexander.

I had no idea why. If anything, I was more attracted to this woman than anyone else. I was more excited for her, more eager to fuck her hard. But the more I wanted her, the more I respected her.

It made no sense.

She stirred her glass and took another drink.

My slacks were tight again. "When did you start your company, Ms. Alexander?"

She set her glass down, her shoulders back. Her olive skin was a perfect tone to complement her black dress. Her collarbone was prominent with how straight she stood. "We're in a bar, Thorn. Call me Autumn."

I hadn't known her first name until that moment. When I looked her up, I typed in her company name. Her name was probably on the screen, but I hadn't noticed it. Now that I'd heard her name, my breathing became slightly strained. It was so simple and so elegant. I could easily picture myself saying it as I came deep inside her. "Autumn." I said her name out loud, testing it out on my tongue. It made me feel like I had a piece of her, could call her something intimate even though it was just a name. "Beautiful name."

"Thanks."

"Thorn."

She nodded. "I know. You're a pretty famous man."

I hoped my celebrity wasn't just based on my scandal with Titan. I did a lot of work for my company, allowed my parents to retire comfortably, and I built companies from the ground up—ones that were immensely successful. I didn't want history to reduce me to a man who'd loved and lost a woman. "Unfortunately."

"It's always lonely at the top. The higher you go, the more people there are to watch you fall."

My eyes narrowed on her face, surprised by the second wise thing she's said. She'd laid out some surprising things that I'd never expected her to say. But then again, this woman operated on a different wavelength. I should stop comparing her to the women I usually hooked up with so I wouldn't be so surprised. "Very true."

She took another drink from her glass, this time, licking her lips.

Now I wondered if she did that on purpose. It was impossible for me not to obsess over that perfect mouth. It would feel so good all over me, from my mouth down to my ball sac. "Are you from New York?"

"Brooklyn."

"Born and raised?" I asked.

"Yes."

"Are your parents still around?"

"Yeah. They live in Connecticut now. They aren't big fans of the city. They prefer the quiet countryside."

"What about you?"

"I prefer the noise. It's what I'm used to."

I couldn't imagine myself living anywhere else but in the heart of Manhattan. The world was going at constant speed, and I loved living in the fast lane. I liked staying out until four a.m. because nothing ever closed in the city that never slept. "They must be proud of you."

"They are." She smiled when she spoke of her parents. "My father was a high school teacher, and my mother took care of the house. Money was always an issue for us. My mother could never work because she has a condition."

I didn't ask what it was because I didn't feel like I had the right to ask. But I'd deduced that they could only afford to move to Connecticut because she took care of them. "What did your father teach?"

"Physics."

"That must be where you get it from."

"Probably," she said with a chuckle. "I always had a private tutor to help me when I came home from school."

"You provide for them?"

She nodded. "They have very comfortable lives now. That makes me happy. They did the best they could, and I'm glad I can repay them after everything they've done for me."

I knew I would do the same for my parents. I was close to my family, so it was something I could relate to. I admired her for doing that because not everyone was so generous. When people had money, it only made them greedy. "Then they must be even more proud of you."

Despite the smile she wore, she shrugged. She never announced her success or bragged about her qualities. She wasn't even conceited about her looks.

She was one of the humblest people I'd ever met. Most people I knew in the business world were successful but also fiercely insecure. They compensated for their fear by bragging even more. The truly successful people said very little about themselves— because they actually wanted to hide their stunning success.

"You're close to your family?" she asked.

If she saw me in the tabloids a lot, then she probably already knew this. "Very."

She gave a slight nod. "That's nice."

"I have a younger brother too. He works in Chicago, so I don't see him a lot. But when we're together, we have a good time."

"I'm an only child."

I drank my scotch. "When did you start your company?"

"Shortly after I dropped out of college. So I was about eighteen at the time. My parents were so angry when I left the university and started working out of a storage shed. But within a year, I made some money and could pay my bills. After that, everything escalated very quickly. I've built on my existing technology and have created some magnificent things."

"What are you working on now?"

She wore a guarded smile. "You know I can't tell you that, Thorn."

I didn't consider our conversation a conflict of interest. I wasn't planning on telling Titan any of this. The real reason I was having this conversation was simply because I wanted to get to know her. "I'm impressed by your work. I can only imagine what goes on in that brain of yours every day."

"I have the same thoughts as anyone else my age. The only reason why I'm unique is because I apply my knowledge differently. That's all."

"I think you're being too humble."

"Or simply too honest." She drank from her glass, and when she set it down, there was a bright lipstick mark around the edge. "Do you like working for your family's company?"

"I don't work for it. I own it." I wasn't on a power trip. I just didn't want her to think I worked under my father or some other family member. My parents had walked away from the company over a decade ago. I'd been the chief operator of it ever since. "My parents are retired, and my brother is more interested in becoming a lawyer."

"My mistake."

I didn't want to sound like a dick, but I didn't want her to get the wrong impression of me. I wasn't some lazy rich boy. I worked hard for my money. I made my family proud of me by the effort I put into preserving our legacy. "And yes, I enjoy it. I've started other companies too, so I have other businesses as well."

"Sometimes I think about branching out, but I don't have much time. I'm needed in the lab."

"And that's why you want to work with Titan?"

"Exactly. I could focus on what I'm good at, and she could focus on what she's good at. Perfect match."

It really was. "I'll talk to her again."

"You will?" she asked, that soft smile on her lips. "You're really pushing for me, huh?"

"I'm not pushing for you—I'm pushing for her. She's a very stubborn woman, and she doesn't go back on her word. But I think she should reconsider this. I see the arrangement as nothing but a benefit to her."

"That's flattering."

"You earned it."

Her eyes fell again, softening in a vulnerable way. When she smiled, she was beautiful. But when she showed this expression, her true feelings, she was undeniably gorgeous.

My cock had hardened so many times that night

I felt a little light-headed. My blood had been redirected to my cock on and off for several hours now—and I wasn't even fucking. The teeth of my fly constantly bit into me, but my thickness was out of my control. This woman had a powerful grip on my dick—without even touching it.

She grabbed her glass and drank the remaining contents. Her lipstick prints were all over the edge now. She seemed to drink from a different spot every single time. She slowly set it down again then looked me in the eye. A long pause ensued, as if she were carefully considering what she was going to say before she said it.

Then she glanced down.

And looked right at the bulge in my slacks.

She lifted her gaze up to me again, her thick eyelashes shifting up as her gaze moved. Her green eyes were filled with confidence—and something else. "Is he like that all the time? Or is that just for me?"

I fought the smile that wanted to stretch across my lips. A shiver moved up my spine, and her directness burrowed under my skin. I was a confident man, and now I realized there was nothing sexier than a confident woman. I forgot to take a breath because I was stunned by her bluntness. She could mention my dick without even blushing, and she obviously wasn't embarrassed to be caught looking. "It's definitely you, sweetheart." My eyes shifted to her mouth, and I wanted to kiss her right then and there. If that wasn't an open invitation to make a move, I didn't know what was. Women had been forward with me before, but never in such a sexy and potent way.

"Now, that *is* flattering." She grabbed my scotch off the counter and downed the rest of it in a single gulp.

I watched her throat shift as she swallowed, imagining her swallowing something else.

She set the glass down, upside down. "My place or yours?"

My smoldering expression intensified at her cool confidence. She wanted me, and she wasn't afraid to get right to the point. She flirted subtly with me, and then she made her intentions bluntly obvious. She could spend the night with any man she wanted— but she wanted me.

Fuck, that was sexy.

I liked a woman who took what she wanted.

And this woman did a perfect job of doing just that. "Depends. Who's closer?"

WE STEPPED INSIDE MY PENTHOUSE, THE TOP FLOOR OF a building overlooking the river. I bought the property almost ten years ago as an investment, and after the economic change over the last decade, it had certainly paid off. But I hadn't sold it because it was a rare piece of property. The view was spectacular, more spectacular than any other penthouse I'd been to.

She sauntered inside, gliding on her heels like she was elevated off the ground. Her eyes swept over my home, taking in the luxurious furniture, gorgeous rug, and the rest of the enormous living room. It was a ten-thousand-square-foot floor, and I had it all to myself. There were four bedrooms in the place, but I didn't have guests very often. At least, not the kind that slept in a different room. She turned back to me when she was finished staring. "You have a nice place."

"Thanks." I slowly walked up to her, all of my restraints slashed away. She was only there for one reason, so I didn't have to be a professional gentleman anymore. The only uncertainty I felt was her position. How would I take her?

My hands finally moved to her hips, feeling the

curves through the soft fabric of her dress. Even in heels, she was much shorter than me. She was a petite woman, but I never viewed her as small. She had the kind of presence that filled every corner of the room.

My fingers felt the fabric in my fingertips, scrunching it up as I gripped her. I felt it slide against her soft skin, felt it against her tight stomach. Once that dress was gone, I knew she would be a beautiful sight to behold. Her olive skin and her sexy curves would drive me crazier than I already was. "I know I should offer you a drink, but I don't want to." My face was close to hers, but I didn't move in with a kiss. I glanced at her plump lips, fantasizing how they would feel against my mouth. The longer I built the anticipation, the better it would feel.

"I don't want a drink." Her hands were pressed to my chest, and they slowly migrated down, over the muscular grooves of my stomach and to my belt. She felt the leather before she moved farther south. While holding my gaze, she placed her fingers over the bulge in my slacks.

I stopped breathing once I felt her fingers against my hard shaft.

She traced the outline with her fingertips, measuring it from the base to the tip. My cock stretched up my slacks at an angle, moving to my opposite hip because there wasn't enough room vertically. I knew I was particularly well-endowed downstairs. I had a cock built to fuck. She glided her palm over it next, her lips parted slightly in excitement. "I want you."

Maybe seeing my big dick was the only reason she wanted to fuck me. She had been cold to me in her office, but the second I stood up and she came into direct contact with it, her attitude changed.

But I didn't give a damn.

If she wanted my big dick, she could have it—all night long.

Autumn looked at me through her thick eyelashes. Then she licked her bottom lip.

The only reason why I hadn't kissed her yet was because I was too busy enjoying this. Her forward-ness was sexy. She wanted my thick cock to make her come all night, and I'd gladly fulfill her expectations. Whatever fantasy she wanted, I would make it happen.

My hand left her hip and slowly moved up past her cheek. My fingers finally came into contact with her dark hair, and I felt the softness brush against me like a rose petal. Her skin was warm to the touch, and as my fingers settled around the back of her neck and under the fall of her hair, I could feel her strong pulse.

I moved my mouth to hers and finally greeted her lips with mine. Soft, plump, and delicious. My breath was sucked out of my mouth as I kissed her, the fiery desire making me tremble. It was a million times better than what I fantasized. Her mouth was warm and soft, and I felt the jolt of electricity spike down my spine.

I gripped her harder with my fingers as I deepened the kiss, our mouths moving together and breaking apart. Her warm breath filled my mouth, and now the smell of her perfume was more potent than before. My hand squeezed her slender waistline, gripping her harder than I meant to.

The speed of our kiss increased, our mouths moving together more rapidly. I couldn't get enough of her, and she couldn't get enough of me. Her tongue moved into my mouth, finding mine in an erotic embrace.

My cock twitched. "Fuck..." I spoke into her mouth, all my coherent thoughts gone. My lifestyle was erotic and taboo. I'd experienced more things than most men could dream of. But I'd never had a kiss like this. I'd never felt my body come to life with such vigor. A woman had never made my hands shake.

Her fingers moved to my belt, and she slowly unfastened it before she moved to my button and fly.

I hadn't taken it a step further because I was still absorbing her kiss. My tongue was still dancing with hers, still enjoying her. I enjoyed her top lip as well as her bottom one. With every passing second, my heart beat even faster.

She unbuttoned the front of my jacket and pushed it off my shoulders so it would fall to the ground behind me.

My slacks were loose around my waist, my cock popping out of the top of my boxers. My fingers gripped her hair and wrapped it around my knuckles, getting a tighter grip on her. The more I had her, the more I wanted her. I didn't want her to slip from my grasp because every inch of her body was officially mine. "I jerked off to you this morning." I spoke into her mouth, no longer possessing a single coherent thought. All I thought about was fucking this woman a million ways. I wanted to make her mine, make her full with my cock. I'd wanted her since the first moment I saw her—and I felt no shame in that.

She sucked my bottom lip before we broke apart,

the same sex-crazed look in her eyes. Her fingers played with my boxers, and she slowly dragged them down my hips. "What was I doing to you?" Her lips moved to the corner of my mouth where she gave me another kiss.

"You were on your knees—sucking my dick." Ever since the first time I'd laid my eyes on her mouth, I'd wanted it wrapped around my cock. I wanted to push my thickness down her tiny throat. I wanted to make her gag around my monster cock. If she expected me to say something romantic, like I wanted to kiss her all over her body instead, then she was in for a surprise.

"Did you come?" She kissed me again, tugging my boxers to my thighs so my cock was free.

"Hard."

She sucked my bottom lip before she slowly lowered herself to her knees.

Jesus Christ.

My chest stiffened when I realized what she was doing. Her knees fell to the hardwood floor, and she flipped her thick hair behind her shoulder. She eyed my cock like sucking it would be nothing but a pleasure.

Both of my hands formed fists.

I couldn't believe this was really happening.

This woman was on her knees—and I didn't even command her to be on her knees.

She wrapped her fingers around my length then looked up at me through her thick eyelashes.

Fuck. My hand slid underneath her hair and wrapped around the back of her neck. I resisted the urge to yank her toward me, knowing she would suck my dick perfectly once she was ready.

She licked her lips.

I was going to come in her face right that instant if she kept this up.

Instead of pushing her mouth over my length, she tilted my cock to the ceiling and pressed her mouth against my balls.

Goddamn.

The second her warm lips were pressed to my sac, I took in a sharp breath. No other pair of lips had ever felt so good. My fingers tightened against the back of her neck, and I narrowed my eyes on her gorgeous face.

She dragged her tongue over my textured skin, tasting my balls. Then she sucked them into her mouth, rubbing her tongue against them with the perfect pressure.

My fingers dug deeper.

Popping sounds emerged as she sucked and

released. She licked her lips then kept going, devouring my balls like she felt privileged to be on her knees right that moment.

I'd never wanted to come so much in my life.

When my balls were soaked, she moved up my base, dragging her sexy tongue all the way to my tip. Then she swiped her tongue over my head, getting the drop of lubrication that seeped from the entrance. It was sticky, and a line of my juice spread between her mouth and the head of my cock.

This was much better than my fantasy.

Her lips finally surrounded my head, and she sucked hard. She wanted to taste more of me, to taste my arousal on her tongue.

My hand moved into her hair, pulling it away from her face. I could watch this performance all day, but my dick wouldn't last that long.

Then she started to move to my base, taking in as much of my length as she could. She stopped over halfway, her mouth gaping open she tried to cram my impressive size deep inside. She pulled off again to take a breath before she moved in again.

Her spit collected on my length then dripped to the floor. She was slathering me in her saliva, priming me so I could fit in her tight little pussy. The lubrication would help, but she was making me so thick it was bound to hurt anyway.

She continued to move her mouth back and forth, her eyes darting to mine from time to time. Tears formed in the corners of her eyes because my size was too big for her to handle, but that didn't slow her down. She kept going, giving me the best head of my life.

If I let this continue, I would explode inside her mouth. My come would sit on her tongue, and I would command her to swallow it. As much as I wanted to finish this fantasy to the very end, I wanted to fuck her more.

I forced myself to pull my dick out of her mouth.

Disappointment filled her eyes, like she wanted to suck me off until she had my come in her belly.

Fuck, she was torture.

I grabbed her by the arm and pulled her to her feet. Before she could take a step, I scooped her into my arms and carried her into my bedroom down the hallway. She was light like I expected, but also perfect in my arms.

I sat her on the bed and unbuttoned my collared shirt. My fingers were focused on unclasping every single button, but my eyes were pinned on the beautiful woman watching me. Instead of looking at the way my shirt opened more and more, her eyes were stuck to mine. Beautiful, green, and vibrant, they were undressing me as much as my own fingers. I could see her desire as well as I could feel my own.

The shirt came undone, and I pulled it off my arms and let it fall onto the floor. Tall and proud, I stood in front of the bed, watching her eyes sweep across my physique. She took in every slab of muscle, every ridge between my abs. Wordlessly, she worshiped my body. I filled out my suits well, made my t-shirts stretch over my biceps and chest. I hit the gym religiously and almost always had a protein shake for lunch. Being in the best physical shape had always been important to me because I never knew when I would need that strength. I'd overpowered Jeremy and stabbed him in the heart, and that was only possible because I was a hundred and eighty pounds of solid muscle. Titan had been shot just because she ruffled someone's feathers. I had to be ready for anything.

Watching Autumn's reaction made all those workouts worth it.

She licked her lips.

She took a deep breath.

Her thighs pressed together.

All the signs of arousal were there. She wanted to fuck me as hard as I wanted to fuck her.

I removed my socks, and I stood completely naked in front of her. Over six feet of chiseled strength and fair skin, I'd seen lots of women look at me the way she did now, but they never meant so much. Getting the look of desire from a woman who could have any man just made me want her more. I wanted to fuck her to please myself, but I wanted to be every fantasy she ever had too.

I grabbed her ankles and lifted them to my chest. The points of her stilettos dug into my skin, but I liked the rough bite. Her dress slowly rose up her thighs, revealing just a peek of her bright pink thong underneath her black dress.

Jesus Christ.

I wrapped my fingers around her slender ankles, and I took a deep breath to steady my excitement. I wanted to tug her legs apart and sink inside her before I fucked her senseless, but I had to slow it down.

I had to take my time.

I wanted to make her so hot, she'd beg me to give it to her.

I turned one of her legs out and kissed the inside of her knee, tasting the soft skin. My tongue rubbed against it gently, and I thought I tasted a hint of vanilla. I slipped off one shoe at the same time, and then dropped the other.

My mouth moved farther up her gorgeous legs, reaching for the sensitive spot in her inner thighs. Her breathing increased the closer I became, becoming increasingly haywire with every passing second. Her chest rose higher, her breaths grew heavier. I kissed both of her thighs then moved farther to the apex of her legs.

Then she stopped breathing altogether.

I kissed the soft fabric of her panties, right over her clit.

The moan she released was the sexiest one I'd ever heard.

I continued to kiss the area, my fingers rubbing her at the same time. I grasped the center of her panties and yanked it over, revealing that soft, pink flesh. My eyes took in her beautiful clit and the slit that was already oozing with arousal. My testosterone spiked, and I placed my mouth against the most delicious pussy I'd ever tasted.

She didn't beg just yet, but it was only a matter of time.

Her fingers dug into my blond hair, and she arched her back, spreading her legs and giving more of herself to me. Her heavy sighs were full of satisfaction but deep desperation. She wanted more—needed more.

I ate her pussy and explored her everywhere. I loved the way she smelled, the way she tasted. I loved feeling her lubrication against my lips, enjoying the sticky thickness. There was no hiding how aroused she was. Her pussy was soaked—and not from my saliva. I blew across her wet opening then sucked her clit into my mouth.

Her hips bucked, and she released a moan that resembled a scream. Her fingers skipped my hair and dug into my scalp. "Thorn..."

She said my name.

Fuck yes.

I fisted her panties in my hand and dragged them down her legs. She lifted her ass to help me, anxious for what was coming next.

I stared at her pussy again, imagining my rock-hard dick inside her. My hand yanked up her dress, and I kissed the smooth skin of her belly. She had a piercing in her navel, and I found that damn sexy. I licked the jewel then explored the tight skin over her abs. She was petite but had a strong core. I moved farther up until I reached the bottom swell of her breasts. I sucked in a breath to smell her then dragged my tongue up her sternum.

I'd never been with such a beautiful woman.

The sexiest woman in the world was on my bed, half naked and soaking wet. She wanted my cock between her legs tonight. There wasn't another man on her mind—just me. She wanted to scream my name, to come all over my dick.

She wanted all of me.

I pulled her dress over her head, finally revealing the gorgeous tits I didn't get to stare at earlier. Just as perky as they seemed in her dress, they were tight and firm. Her nipples were hard and begging to be sucked between my teeth.

I couldn't hold myself back. I pressed my face right into her valley, and I dragged my tongue right between her tits. My tongue explored her gorgeous skin, and I sucked and kissed her everywhere. When I got to her nipples, I was more than rough. My large palm gripped and squeezed one tit while I ravaged her other tit. The scruff along my jaw brushed against her delicate skin, making her nipples harden even more.

Fuck, I wanted to do this all night.

I held my body on top of hers, my arms pinned on either side of her body. My weight pushed her into the mattress, and I covered every inch of her gorgeous skin with mine. She was mine now. Until the sun rose the following morning, she was staying right there.

I wanted to fuck her from behind so I could stare at that gorgeous asshole. I wanted to have her ride me while I sat against the headboard. I wanted to take her a million ways. But right now, I wanted her legs spread wide for me as I fucked her into the mattress. I wanted to conquer her, to make her legs shake as I brought her to climax over and over. I wanted to stuff her gorgeous pussy with my big dick until she was too sore to handle more.

Her hands slid up my chest as she looked at me with eyes lit up like Christmas lights. Her dark hair was spread across the pillow, and her tits were tight and firm. With her gaze settled on mine, she spread her legs then hooked them around my waist. Her soft fingers moved underneath my arms, and she hooked her arms around my shoulders. "Are you going to fuck me, Thorn?" Her eyes kept a steady look of confidence, and her lips parted like she was desperate for my kiss.

I pressed my cock against her wet folds and slowly ground against her. "When you beg me to." Skin-to-skin, I ground my wet cock against her slick clit. My shaft picked up lubrication from her slit, and I rubbed it across her swollen nub. I moved harder as I angled my neck down and kissed her.

I couldn't wait to be inside her.

But I wanted this amazing woman to want me as badly as I wanted her.

Her nails dug into my back, and she breathed into my mouth as I pressed her into the mattress. She jerked forward and backward as I picked up momentum, my cock pressing against her and my lips devouring her. Her breaths turned to moans, and those moans quickly escalated into something more. She yanked me into her with her legs and dug her nails harder until she nearly drew blood.

I could feel her breathing escalate, feel her tremble. She was a proud woman who didn't beg for anything, but that was about to change. I wanted her to melt for me, to realize I was the best lay she was ever going to find. I wanted her to think of me every time she fucked someone else, to wish I were the man fucking her instead.

A few minutes later, she cracked. "Thorn...fuck me."

I sucked her bottom lip. "Beg."

She dragged her nails all the way to my ass, my

cock rubbing against her harder. "Please...please fuck me."

I watched the redness flush her cheeks as she ventured into the realm of pleasure. She was about to climax—and I wasn't even inside her yet.

Her eyes stared into mine, her lips open so her moans could emerge. "Please..."

Now I was about to burst. I pulled my length away from her throbbing pussy and grabbed a condom from the nightstand drawer. I ripped it open quickly and rolled it onto my length, using the magnum size because my package was far bigger than average. Once the latex was secured around my base, I pushed my head inside her.

She didn't take me right away. Her pussy was small like the rest of her, and no matter how wet she was, I was a big man to handle. She bit her bottom lip as I slowly pushed farther inside her, stretching her channel apart to make room for myself.

I slowly sank into her, my monster cock forcing its way inside.

Her hands moved back to my shoulders, and she clung to me tightly, breathing hard in reaction to my entrance into her tightness.

I pinned one of her legs back, opening her wider so I could get the rest inside. I pushed as far as I could go and left a few inches out, but it was still the best pussy I'd ever had. So wet, so warm...fucking perfect.

Her tits rose to the ceiling with every breath she took, and she gripped me tighter than before. Her mouth was wide open as she breathed, and her pants were the sexiest thing I'd ever heard. "God... you have a big dick."

I thrust my hips and fucked her at a steady pace. My body ached to fuck her as aggressively as I could, but I knew her tiny channel couldn't handle that just yet. She was still molding to my length, getting used to the profound stretching.

I already wanted to come. I could feel the heat in my groin, the fire that started just before the explosion. Watching this beautiful woman take my dick was the sexiest thing in the world. It was an image I would beat off to over and over.

Her hands moved to my chest, and she started to rock her hips with me, taking my thickness a little easier. Her breathing turned irregular, her moans became incoherent words. She closed her eyes for a moment and bit her bottom lip, feeling the beginning of a prominent burst of ecstasy.

"Eyes on me."

She opened her eyes and locked her gaze on

mine. Her tits shook with the thrusts, and her ankle hooked around my leg. "God, I'm going to come..."

I'd been inside her for a barely few minutes, and she was already crumbling. My cock was hitting her in all the right places, and I was pleasing her the way every man should please a woman.

Her fingers wrapped around my biceps as she was swept away in the thrill of passion. Her moans erupted in my face, and her perfect pussy tightened around my rock-hard cock even more. Her cream sheathed the condom all the way to the base, and she rode the powerful high I gave her. Her back arched, her head rolled back, and her nipples became so hard they were pointier than the tip of a sharpened pencil. "Yes...yes." High-pitched and broken, her voice trailed off. Her expression mirrored a look of tearful joy. She crumbled underneath me, fascinating me with the way she writhed from the orgasm I just gave her. "So good..."

My mind lost focus as my carnal instincts took over. I had just seen a gorgeous woman put on an erotic performance, and now my dick couldn't be controlled. I wanted to fill the tip of the condom and pretend I was pumping it directly inside her pussy. My breathing became labored, and my balls tightened against my body. The explosion had already been initiated, and there was nothing I could do to stop it. I rode it hard, feeling the come shoot out of my dick with a wave of indescribable pleasure.

I shoved myself deep inside her, only leaving out a few inches because I didn't want to hurt her. I dumped my load inside the condom and stared at the gorgeous woman underneath me. Ever since I'd set eyes on her, I'd wanted to fuck her just like this. It was so good that I wasn't sure if it was truly real.

My balls relaxed again as the dream faded away. The tenderness spread throughout my body, and the wave of satisfaction hit me like a ton of bricks. Fucking her was a million times better than I expected.

I had to fuck her again—just like that.

I slowly pulled out of her, her sticky pussy juice surrounding the used condom. The tip of it was filled with so much white come I thought it would stretch the latex until it ripped.

Autumn stared at me with the same arousal, as if she hadn't just been fucked good and hard. "Fuck me again." She propped herself up on one elbow and kissed my neck, her tongue exploring my shoulder and collarbone. She turned her lips to my ear and breathed into my canal. "Please."

I'd just had a powerful orgasm, the kind that

would knock me out and give me a great night of rest. But those sexy words completely erased my fatigue. She commanded me to pleasure her again—and I'd give this woman whatever she wanted.

I rolled on a new condom and moved on top of her again. "I'm going to fuck you all night, Autumn."

My body was wrapped around hers, my hard chest rising against her soft back every time I took a breath. My crotch was pressed against her ass, my soft dick pressed in between her ass cheeks. I had my arm hooked around her slender waist, keeping right against me throughout the night.

The sex had lasted for a few hours until we were both spent and satisfied. She fell asleep first, and I followed her shortly afterward. Now we were surrounded by the darkness and my soft sheets. My face was pressed into her hair, and I smelled a field of flowers every time I took a breath. My powerful body flooded the sheets with constant heat, keeping her warm beside me.

It was the most comfortable I'd ever been.

Then she stirred, sitting up in bed and making my arm slide away. She ran her fingers through her hair, sighed, and then moved toward the edge of the bed.

I stared at her spine, seeing the tight muscles on either side of the bone. She had a deep curve in her lower back, petite shoulders, and gorgeous hair that trailed halfway down her back.

I didn't drag her back toward me because the sight was so beautiful. It was dark, but I could still make out the features of her body. I could still see a few freckles on her right shoulder. Her wide hips curved into a beautiful waistline. The curve of the outside of her breasts was noticeable in the dim light. She was an amazing woman packed with curves everywhere.

Gorgeous.

She scooted to the edge and prepared to stand up.

"Where do you think you're going?" My large hand could wrap around her wrist twice because she was so small. I secured my hold on her and slowly dragged her back toward me.

She didn't fight it, turning toward me so her tits were visible. "Home."

"It's only..." I squinted as I looked at the alarm clock on my nightstand. "Jesus, it's five in the morning on a Sunday. Get your ass back here." I tugged on her harder, forcing her closer to me.

She smiled as she looked down at me, the exhaustion in her eyes. "I have a lot of stuff to do today. I thought I could sneak out without waking you."

"You're one of those women, huh?" I pulled her on top of me, her luscious tits pressing against my chest. I cupped her cheek then tucked her hair behind her ear. My eyes were heavy with sleep, but I kept them open so I could look at this fine woman.

"What kind of women are we talking about here?"

"That slip out before the sun rises." My fingers moved down her neck and over her chest until I palmed her tit.

"Yes."

"Well, you don't have to do that with me. You can leave when you want, and I won't make you stay."

She smiled. "What are you doing right now?"

"That's different. It's not even morning yet. Now, go back to sleep."

She stared at me as she considered it, her green eyes shifting back and forth slightly as she looked into mine. "I'm having breakfast with someone, and I still need to hit the gym first."

A woman didn't have an ass like that without working hard. I wanted to make another argument to get her to stay, but she had obviously made up her mind. We had a great night of fucking, and now it was back to reality. That was exactly how I wanted it anyway—to resume our professional relationship. "Let me walk you out."

"No." She pushed my chest so I would remain against the mattress. "I know the way." She leaned down and kissed me on the mouth, giving me a slow and seductive kiss.

My hand fisted her hair, and I breathed deeper into her mouth. Every time she kissed me, I felt such a profound sense of passion and desire. I couldn't get enough of her. This woman kissed as good as she fucked.

My cock hardened to the size of a bat under the sheets and pressed against her. Anytime I was in the same room with her, my cock ballooned with eagerness. I saw beautiful women on a daily basis without getting hard. I'd been to strip clubs without being impressed. But with Autumn, my cock was a fucking machine.

She pulled the sheets away then gave me a few pumps with her fingers.

Now I knew she wasn't leaving—unless she was the biggest tease in the world.

She broke our kiss then stuck my dick in her mouth, soaking it until it was coated with her saliva. Then she crawled on top of me and straddled my hips.

Fuck yes.

She found a condom in my nightstand and rolled it onto my length, her fingers working my large length as her eyes stared at it with greed.

My hands gripped her ass. "I'm surprised you aren't too sore."

"I am." She rose onto the balls of her feet then slowly sheathed me. "But you'll make me come anyway."

10

VINCENT

I SAW Thorn across the room talking to Autumn Alexander, one of the brightest minds of our young generation. Her developments in solar and renewable energy were beyond impressive. But judging by the way Thorn was standing so close to her, I suspected they weren't talking about business.

I kept business and pleasure separate. The kind of women I went for had nothing to do with this world. They were usually models. In fact, they were *all* models. They were primarily foreign too, holding citizenship from France or Italy.

I guess I had a type.

My last relationship ended unexpectedly. After my conversation with Titan, I reevaluated my life. Even with a woman by my side and in between my sheets, my existence was utterly empty. Despite the company, I was still lonely.

My conversations were meaningless and drab. Most of the time they talked and I just listened. That wasn't their fault.

I just didn't say much.

I took the strong and silent type to a whole new level.

Women liked me because I was rich, sophisticated, had great taste in wine and art—and I had a few yachts.

Women loved yachts.

And I was still handsome.

I started good habits when I was young, eating right and exercising regularly. That benefited me in the long term.

I was young when I had Diesel. I was twenty-one at the time. My wife was the same age. Now I was fifty-six, but I felt much younger than my age indicated. My lean and toned body shaved off ten years to my appearance. If it weren't well known that Diesel was my son, people would mistake him for my brother.

Titan was right—I was still young.

I had a long life ahead of me. Even I lived to be eighty, that still gave me another twenty-five years.

How should I spend it?

The idea of falling in love again didn't sound appealing to me. How could I ever love someone again after the way I loved my wife? She was perfect for me, my better half. I always wondered what she would look like now—if she'd survived. I imagined us cruising the Mediterranean together, still happy and in love.

But she was gone.

I was happy I had my son back, but I was still miserable. I had all the money in the world, but that didn't mean anything to me.

I had no one to share it with.

Isabella would want me to move on. She would have expected me to move on a few years after she passed away. Within the blink of an eye, more than ten years had passed. I hadn't fallen in love with anyone, but I had purposely prevented that from happening.

I only chose women I was attracted to—not ones I cared about.

Maybe it was time for me to move forward.

Or maybe I could never move forward.

I really didn't know.

I mingled with more associates and plastered a fake smile on my face. A young woman touched me on the arm too many times, obviously fishing for my affection. But I wasn't interested.

I didn't say goodnight to Thorn before I left because he seemed absorbed in his conversation with Autumn. I suspected their conversation would continue—probably at his penthouse.

So I went home—alone.

———

CHEYENNE HAD BEEN WORKING FOR ME SINCE THE beginning. She was a few years older than me, and she loved being my executive assistant so much that she never left. I paid her handsomely because my world would fall apart if she ever left. From the way I took my coffee to my most complicated schedules, she had it all figured out.

And Isabella had always liked her.

I guessed Cheyenne reminded me of simpler times, when Isabella would come visit me at the office with Brett and Diesel holding each of her hands. Her visits always distracted me and I ended up staying an extra hour to catch up, but I couldn't refuse seeing my wife in the middle of the day.

I never got tired of her.

Cheyenne walked into my office and set a mug of

coffee on the table—black. "I have the editor in chief of *Platform* on line one. Scarlet Blackwood. She wants to know if you'd be interested in doing a special fashion line for her men's formal wear. She'd also like an interview."

Platform was on every newsstand I passed in Manhattan. It was the biggest fashion magazine in the country, and the only reason why I knew that was because some of my girlfriends had been on the covers. I didn't care about fashion and I had a designer pick out my clothes for me, but publicity was always important. The more celebrity I had, the better my businesses performed. Also, I was working on repairing my image in the media. It took a dive once Diesel spread our story across every front page in the country.

Cheyenne stared at me with a folder tucked under her arm. She wore a cream jacket with matching slacks. She'd just had her first grandchild a few months ago. "You want to take it, or should I get rid of her?"

I suspected I would have my first grandchild soon, now that Diesel was marrying Tatum. I wished Isabella could be alive for that moment. "I'll take it. When's my next meeting?"

"Two hours."

Then I had time. "Put her through."

Cheyenne pressed the phone to her ear. "Please hold for Mr. Hunt." She handed the phone over.

I took it and watched her walk out of my office. "Mrs. Blackwood, how are you?" I didn't know anything about this woman, but her reputation preceded her. Anyone who ran a fashion magazine of that caliber must be phenomenal at her job.

"It's Ms. Blackwood," she said curtly. "And I'm very well now that I have your attention."

I didn't know why, but something about her tone made me smile.

"I'd really love to do a spread about you, Mr. Hunt. I have a few suits that would look magnificent on you. You have a strong following, and you're the leading example of a powerful businessman. Men and women are both fascinated by you."

"I don't know about that, but you flatter me anyway." I smoothed my tie down the front of my chest, feeling the silk against my callused fingertips.

"Can we meet to discuss it further? I'd love to share my ideas with you."

I wasn't big on talking, but I could pose for a few pictures. I'd been photographed a lot in my life. I'd done a few endorsements for Connor Suede, and that always increased my visibility. I'd been associated with a lot of different brands, from luxury cars, jets, and fashion. "I'm interested. But I do have to make something clear."

"Yes?" She had a deep voice that was naturally smoky and sultry. In my mind, I imagined her to be a woman with dark hair. To be the editor in chief of such a respected magazine, she must have years of experience under her belt, but her voice didn't show her age. She sounded the same age as Tatum.

"I'm willing to do an interview, but there are some subjects I won't discuss." My private life was exactly what it was—private. I wasn't interested in discussing the death of my late wife, and I wasn't interested in defending myself against Diesel's previous claims. Business was the only safe subject.

"I understand, Mr. Hunt. Nothing gets printed without your consent."

Some publications weren't so respectful. They would trick you into saying something you regretted just to get more readers. I'd learned to avoid those kinds of tabloids a long time ago, but my guard was always up anyway. "I appreciate that."

"Thank you for your time, Mr. Hunt. We'll talk soon."

Most of my conversations didn't flow well because I wanted to end them as quickly as possible.

But for a stranger, she was surprisingly easy to speak to. She got right to the point and didn't interject pointless blabber. "Goodbye, Ms. Blackwood."

SCARLET BLACKWOOD WASN'T WHAT I EXPECTED.

She walked into the restaurant shortly after noon, wearing a taupe skirt that flared around her hips with a white blouse that hugged her slender waistline. Nude heels were on her feet, and a black blazer with large buttons covered her shoulders. She was decorated with accessories, a gold watch, a diamond necklace, and bangle bracelets. She strutted into the restaurant like it was a runway, her clutch tucked under her arm.

She was definitely part of the fashion world.

Her dark hair was exactly as I pictured it, deep like midnight and shiny. It was pinned away from her face, but the strands were loose enough that the look softened her features. With high cheekbones, almond-shaped eyes, and a slender neck, she possessed all the beauty of the models that hit the runway. But she had something they didn't.

Experience.

It was difficult to discern her age, but she wasn't

in her twenties. She must be her in her late thirties or early forties. There were faint lines in the corners of her eyes and mouth, but her obvious beauty wasn't diminished by her age. A lot of women in the industry resorted to plastic surgery because they needed to retain their looks as long as possible, but Scarlet Blackwood hadn't. She had aged gracefully on her own, obviously taking care of her skin and physique in natural ways.

I noticed all of those things in a matter of thirty seconds. She approached my table with a soft smile on her lips, confidence but also genuineness in her look.

I rose to my feet and extended my hand. "Nice to see you, Ms. Blackwood."

"The pleasure is mine, Mr. Hunt." She squeezed my hand with the same strength before she dropped it. "I appreciate your time. I understand you have a lot going on in your life right now."

I pulled out her chair for her before I moved to the other side of the table.

She paused for just an instant, seemingly caught off guard by my politeness. Then she sat down and placed her clutch in her lap. Self-assured, she possessed a professional charm that was innately comfortable. "I hope Ms. Titan is having a successful recovery. It's an absolute travesty what happened to her. I'm glad she shot that horrible man, but I also wish he was rotting in jail for the rest of his life." The sincerity in her voice was unmistakable. It didn't seem like she was just trying to find something to talk about. She was invested in the story, probably because it was on every news station nearly all of the time. People had pestered me for an interview, but I always declined.

"She's doing very well. She just left the hospital recently, and the rest of her recovery is taking place at home. She's up and about, and the pain is manageable. But she's not in good enough shape to head back to work."

"Of course not. But I'm glad to hear she's back on her feet. I met her once a few years ago. Very nice woman."

"She's incredible." The pride that I felt for my own sons had extended to Tatum. I'd seen her as a daughter long before she agreed to marry my son. There was something about her that resonated with me. Isabella had always wanted a daughter, but it had never happened for us. Perhaps that was why I felt such a connection with Tatum. She also reminded me of Isabella in a lot of ways. If I had a daughter, I imagined she'd be a lot like Tatum.

"You're fond of her?" She tilted her head slightly, a smile on her lips.

"My son couldn't have picked anyone better." I meant that from the bottom of my heart.

Her eyes roamed over my face before her smile faded away. There was still a spark in her eyes, a light that naturally glowed even if the sun was gone. "Diesel is wonderful too. I did a spread with him a few years back. Easy to work with and always respectful."

"That's how he was raised." I'd raised all of my sons to be powerful men, but Isabella had given them everything else they needed, like compassion, respect, and gentleness.

"It sounds like a perfect arrangement. But it's terrible their happiness has been put on hold because of this tragedy."

"It is. But that won't stop them for long." I'd known of Diesel's love for Tatum long before he ever spoke it. Anytime they were in the same room together, his eyes were constantly on her. I could feel his adoration even in a crowded room filled with hundreds of people. It was intense, powerful, and unyielding.

"I'm sure it won't."

The waiter arrived and took our drink orders as

well as our entrée selections. He disappeared a moment later, leaving us to nothing but our conversation. I dealt with people one-on-one like this all of the time, but something about Scarlet made me feel a little different. I wasn't necessarily uncomfortable, but the obvious comfort was the culprit for my rigidness. "What are your ideas, Scarlet?" The introductions had been made, and she'd broken the ice talking about my family. She hadn't mentioned my estrangement with Diesel, but that didn't mean it wasn't further down on her list.

She sat with perfect posture, holding herself like she could be photographed any moment. She removed her black jacket from her shoulders and placed it over the back of the chair. She had slender arms, rounded shoulders, and a feminine collarbone. "I received a new line of suits from one of my favorite designers, and they're so magnificent. I wanted to showcase them in a powerful way, and I couldn't think of a better man to show them off. *Platform* obviously targets a female audience, but that audience consists of personal shoppers, designers, and wives. When they see a man like you showing them off, it'll be a big hit. Not to mention, you're one of the most fascinating bachelors in the world."

I didn't consider myself to be a bachelor, not when I wasn't interested in marriage.

She pulled her phone out of her clutch, and her fingers started tapping against the screen. "I would have brought one here today, but I didn't think it was the best location with all the food hanging around..." She turned the phone around and showed me the screen. "The fabric is unlike anything on the market. It's so strong but so light. You'll never have to worry about breaking a sweat when you walk to work on a summer day."

I never walked to work.

"The simple design is one of its strongest details. It allows the owner of the suit to put out the statement, the vibe. When placed on a man with your musculature, this fabric will mold to your body, almost like a t-shirt. I really hope they design some dresses or skirts soon, because I'd love to have something I could enjoy myself."

I took the phone and examined the image more closely. I zoomed in so I could see the dark fabric and the quality of the buttons. The lighting from the back of the phone changed the appearance of the suit slightly, but once I saw it in person, I would have a better view. But honestly, I didn't care much about clothes or fashion. I wore the nicest attire on the market, whether I personally liked it or not. I didn't care about the clothes, just the statement they created. A soldier always carried his best weapon when he went into battle. When I stepped into a meeting, my suit was my strongest weapon. It protected me like armor, and it projected a web of defense.

She took the phone back and returned it to her clutch. "What do you think?"

"It's nice." I didn't have the interest to say much more than that. Scarlet Blackwood could go into endless detail about just the fabric alone, but I didn't share her same passion. On top of that, I was a man of very few words. I'd always been that way. Isabella used to tease me for it, but she never asked me to change. She adopted my form of communication, which was a wordless conversation.

Scarlet didn't seem disappointed by my short response. "I thought we could get a few shots in the ideal location, perhaps along the French Riviera or Verona, Italy. Something exotic, if you have the availability, of course."

I'd assumed we would do this in a studio. "I don't mind making the trip, but I don't feel comfortable leaving my son behind when he's going through this difficult time."

She pressed her lips together tightly and closed her eyes for just an instant. "Of course...I completely understand. That was an insensitive thing for me to ask."

"It's fine." Diesel and Tatum probably didn't need me, but I wanted to be there if something came up, even if it was just picking up groceries. I hadn't been there for my son for the last ten years, and now I was committed to being by his side every single day for the rest of my life.

"We can do something local. There are lots of beautiful places right in our backyard."

"That would be preferable."

"Great. I'll set everything up with your assistant."

I gave a nod, my eyes set on her face. Her skin was darker than mine, with a natural tan that gave her a beautiful complexion. She had dark eyes as well, similar to my own. She had an innately exotic look to her, like she could be from Milan or Southern Italy. She didn't possess a trace of an accent, so it didn't seem like she'd relocated here. But her unique appearance caused me to stare— even more than I usually did.

"Now for the part you aren't looking forward to..." She pulled out the tape recorder and set it on the table. "I promise I'll make this painless if you trust me."

No one had ever asked me to trust them. Trust wasn't something that was given within a few conversations. It was earned over a lifetime, and even then, trust wasn't guaranteed. Perhaps she and I had different definitions of the word. "I like painless."

"The objective of the article is to flatter you. I want to paint you as the powerhouse billionaire whose reputation precedes you. But every other paper has written about your financial triumphs a million times...so I want more. I want the man underneath the suit. I want the vulnerability that doesn't ruin your strength. I think people will find that much more interesting, and they'll respect you even more."

I didn't do vulnerability. I didn't do emotion. Very few people saw that deeper side of me, and the only people who witnessed it were my family. I wore my heart on my sleeve with Diesel and Tatum because it was necessary. I now told Brett things I should have told him a long time ago. When it came to them, there was no holding back. But the world didn't deserve the same from me. "No one other outlet has ever written a piece like that because it's not something I'm interested in. I do my job, make my money, and then go home. I'm not obligated to share every thought, every feeling, with anyone." I held her gaze despite the cold statement I'd just made. She seemed like a woman with good intentions. She was honest and up front, and I appreciated that. But didn't mean I would give her what she wanted.

She didn't show a single reaction, obviously unaffected by my callous response. "Mr. Hunt, you're the one driving this car. We can go in any direction you choose. I'm just the tour guide. But I think an article like this would be beneficial to you. I understand you don't want to share every aspect of your life with readers or strangers because it's none of their business. Your personal life is separate from your business enterprise. But the world always watches every move you make. They're fascinated by your success, your looks, and your presence. They're hungry for more of you, regardless. At least now you can give them a piece of yourself—on your own terms. I don't need to mention the problems with Diesel because it's already the elephant in the room. You don't need to defend your side of the story, but you could explain it. This is an opportunity for you for to increase your standing, to show the world that the man underneath the suit is just as powerful as the man who wears it.

That's just my advice...but you can do whatever you want."

It was the second time she'd pushed me, but she didn't cross the line and override my power. A lot of things she mentioned were true. People were obsessed with me. They were sharing gossip instead of facts. At least I could set the record straight.

"You can give me a list of topics that are off-limits. I won't ask you about them." She pulled a small notepad out of her purse with a pen. "Then we'll start the interview." She held the pen to the paper. "So what are they, Mr. Hunt?"

My eyes shifted to her slender hand, seeing the tight skin. Her age didn't show in her hands, only in subtle places in her face. I turned my gaze back to her, seeing the dark eyes that were filled with gentle power. "My late wife. She's off-limits." She was the love of my life, and I didn't discuss something so personal with anyone. Even my own sons rarely heard me mention her. Losing her was the hardest suffering I'd ever endured. It'd been over a decade, but I'd never gotten over it. My memories of her and our life together were mine. I guarded them greedily, like they were buried treasure.

Scarlet didn't hesitate before she made her note. "Anything else?"

I was willing to discuss anything else but Isabela. She was the only thing I couldn't compromise on. Nothing else seemed to matter. "No."

Her eyebrow rose slightly, and she set her pen down. "Thank you for trusting me, Mr. Hunt."

I wasn't sure why I did.

She grabbed the recorder and pressed her thumb into the button. It started to record. "You're one of the top ten richest people in the world with a net worth of over sixty billion dollars. It's the kind of success most people will never even dream of. What has been the biggest contributor to your success?"

It was a stale question, the kind I got all the time. "I worked hard. Before I went to college, I knew I wanted to be an entrepreneur. I'd been fascinated by business, but not just running a company or working for one. I wanted to start something that would live long after I died. I wanted to be remembered for something. Immortality is something that motivates a great deal. I work so hard in life to secure my station in death."

The waiter brought our drinks then walked off again. Scarlet didn't react to his presence, her eyes glued to mine. She must have anticipated my answer, but she still seemed genuinely interested by it. "What do you love most about it? And what do you hate the most?"

"I love the power. When I want something, I get it. People are aware of my presence the instant I walk into a room. I have the ability to make anything happen. But, as they say, with great power comes great responsibility. I think I handle that well. What I hate most is being in the public eye. People think they know me based on who I'm dating or what suit I wear. Honestly, no one really knows me."

Scarlet didn't touch her glass of wine. It was deep red, almost purple. I wondered if she would leave a lipstick mark once she took a drink. It was a stupid thought to have, and I didn't know why I had it. She seemed more interested in me than taking a drink. "You're very particular about your suits. It's rumored that you never wear the same one twice. Is that true?"

"Yes."

"Why is that?"

"My suits are my image. They heighten my presence and exemplify my power. They also complement my mood. I never feel the same way on any given day, so I never wear the same suit. They're my most important possession, and they can change the outcome of business indirectly. There's no greater feeling than putting on a new suit, still crisp from the designer. That's a luxury I allow myself."

"And what do you do with the suits once you're done wearing them?"

"Donate them."

She slightly nodded before she finally took a drink. Lipstick smeared on the glass, deep red like blood. She set it down again, her slender fingers wrapped around the stem. "Where do you donate them?"

"The United War Veterans Council. They distribute them to vets and other people looking for work. They wear them to their interviews. It's part of their rehabilitation program. And like I said before, the right suit can make you feel like you're worth billions—even if you aren't. It can change the game, change your confidence."

She didn't pull out a list of notes during our interview. In fact, it felt more like a conversation than an interrogation. Scarlet didn't seem like an editor getting a story her readers would want to read. She seemed like someone who wanted the truth— not some romanticized lie. Perhaps that was why *Platform* had the biggest list of subscribers in the media world.

"Your sons, Diesel and Jax Hunt, have followed

in your footsteps. Did you push them to be successful businessmen as well? Or was that something they cultivated on their own?"

People usually asked questions about my own success. They didn't seem to care about my relationship with my two sons. We were very different people. "I've always been close to Diesel and Jax. Once they became adults, our relationship shifted from parent and child and turned into a friendship. I know both of them look up to me in a lot of ways, and I suspect I have a lot to do with their motivations. But honestly, I pushed them a lot too. It was important to me to raise fine men, the kind of men that could stand on their own two feet and take care of their own family. Not only did I succeed, but they exceeded all of my expectations. They're much better versions of myself."

Scarlet gave me a smile. "You sound proud."

"I'm proud of all my sons—especially Brett." I didn't talk about him much, and I needed to do it more. He carried a different last name, but he was a member of my family. Brett and I had started a new relationship, but we still had a lot of work to do. "He started from nothing. I didn't help him with his business, and he figured out a way to achieve his goals on his own. Now he's one of the biggest car designers in the industry, and he's made millions."

"Diesel told his version of your broken relationship a few months ago. You've obviously made up and have moved forward, which is great to hear. But is there anything else you'd like to share? Has that experience taught you something that you can impart to others? Family is the most important thing in the world—but it can also be the most toxic."

She put it beautifully. Some families were perfect and didn't have a single bump in the road, but most weren't like that. There were difficult times, horrifying times. "My estrangement from my son had nothing to do with love. I've always loved him with everything I have. I'd sacrifice my life for his in a heartbeat. I still remember the first time I held him in my arms. It's hard to believe he was ever that small considering his size now...he's just as big as I am. Our separation was entirely my fault, and I admit that with no shame."

"Would you mind telling us what happened?"

"Diesel's story isn't far from the truth. I didn't treat Brett with the love he deserved. It drove him away, and it also pushed Diesel away as well. He didn't tolerate my treatment of Brett, so he left. I'm proud of him for the decision he made. He stood up for someone when he could have taken the easy way out—but he didn't." My life would have been so different if I hadn't let my jealousy and pain get to me. But I had, and this was my reality.

"I loved my wife in a way I can never explain. Our relationship was intense, beautiful...and so many other things. My love for her made me a very jealous man. Knowing she'd loved someone else had always tortured me. Knowing she'd been with someone else when we could have had more time together always haunted me. So I resented Brett because of it...she made him with another man she loved. I should have taken him in as my own, but that's not what happened. It was impossible for me to look at him at not think of his father..." My eyes remained trained on hers even though the tension filled the air between us. I was brutally honest with my confession, no longer caring what people thought of me. I'd committed my actions, and now I had to face the consequences. "I realized how wrong I was and I've worked to repair my relationship with him. He's a man now, old enough that he doesn't need a father. But I want him in my life. It's not just because my wife is disappointed in me. It's because I want to get back the time we lost."

"Thank you for sharing. You sound like a father who's willing to do anything for his family."

"I am—even if that means admitting I was wrong. Before I had kids, I imagined having a family would be easy. It would be simple and fulfilling. But as I aged, I realized being a parent is the most difficult job you'll ever have. It's unpredictable, heartbreaking, and stressful. I've made a lot of mistakes, despite my experience in so many other areas. Nothing in life would have prepared me for the venture. Being a single parent only made the task even more difficult. But all I can do is apologize for my mistakes and never give up. I love my sons more than life itself, and I'm committed to being everything they need—at every stage of their lives. I won't repeat my mistakes, and I'm going to enjoy every minute I have left with them. For other parents out there, times can be difficult. But it's also the most rewarding thing you'll ever do."

She hung on to my words even when I'd finished speaking. She gave a slight nod, her expression hard as she concentrated on my face. "Well said, Mr. Hunt. I have a daughter, and it's been good as well as bad."

"How old is she?"

"She's a junior in college. I had her very young…"

I was curious to know how old she was, but it felt like an inappropriate question. "Then I'm sure you understand."

"Yes...I do." She sipped her wine again, taking a bigger drink this time. "Were you surprised when Diesel told you he was engaged to Tatum Titan?"

"No." I was the one who pushed him to marry her. "And he made the best decision of his life."

"Sounds like you've already welcomed her into the family."

"Yes. She already feels like a daughter."

"The shooting rocked the entire nation...how has it affected you?"

It affected me in a million ways. Tatum was a wonderful person who didn't deserve that, and my son didn't deserve to be in pain. It was so chilling it froze me right down to the bone. "The incident has shed light on the way some men still view women. Bruce Carol's vendetta only shows that some men refuse to give a professional woman the respect she deserves. If he can't beat her, then he needs to destroy her. Instead of acknowledging that the better businessperson won, he hated her for her fierce intelligence. He wanted her to be prey—and stay prey. It's sickening, and I'm glad Tatum killed him." It was a risky thing to say in an interview, but I didn't care. I didn't care how that statement would make Mrs. Carol feel or her children. If Tatum hadn't killed him first, she'd be the one in a graveyard. "I'm proud of her for the way she handled the situation. Not too many people would have had the courage to stare down their gunman the way she stared him down. And even when she was bleeding out of her chest, she didn't stop fighting. She kept going until she won. She's a role model to all of us—not just women. It's difficult for me to see such a strong person confined to a bed, to know they're fighting for their life in surgery as I sit in the waiting room. But her recovery has been remarkable, and it just shows that the darkness can't last forever. The light will return—and it'll shine brighter than it did before." I was proud of Tatum for continuing to live her life with the same dignity as before. She didn't flinch at loud noises, and she wasn't afraid to go back to work. She refused to let the trauma affect her mental state of being, and she obviously didn't feel any remorse for taking a man's life—not that she should. I was proud of her in the way every father should be proud of his daughter. She refused to be the victim —and she did it with grace.

Scarlet watched me for a long time, letting my final response fill the air. She didn't ask another question, and when she reached for the recorder on the table, I knew the interview was over. "Thank you, Mr. Hunt. I think our readers will be fascinated by this story—I know I am." She placed the recorder in her clutch then cleared her throat. "I'll have my crew contact your team to set up the photo shoot. And I'll give you my article before I publish it, just to make sure you approve of it."

No one had ever offered that to me before. "Thank you."

"Thank you for your time, Mr. Hunt. I know you're a very busy man." She prepared to stand up.

We hadn't gotten our lunch yet, and normally, that wouldn't matter to me. The sooner I could leave, the better. Pointless conversations about work never ceased to bore me. But my body stayed in the chair because I didn't want to leave. "Have somewhere to be?"

"No. But I'm sure you do." She stood up, a strand of hair coming loose and falling in front of her face.

I nodded back to the chair. "Have lunch with me."

"Are you sure?" She opened her clutch and prepared to put the cash on the table for the meal she never received.

If she sat down again, a conversation would

ensue. I could go back to my office and get some work done so I could go home early, but I wanted to stay in that exact spot. It was the first time I wanted to have a conversation—even if it was pointless. Even with my ladies, I didn't spend much time talking to them. Sometimes they talked and I listened, but it was usually with partially deaf ears.

But I wanted her to stay. "I'm sure."

11

DIESEL

Her wrists were so slender, so soft. I kissed the inside of each one before I raised them above her head. Her black panties were wet—soaked because of me. I wrapped the lace around her wrists before I secured them to the headboard.

Now she couldn't go anywhere.

No one could take her away from me.

She lay on her back, her firm tits pointed right at me. The skin of her chest was flushed pink, and her eyes showed the same desire that was throbbing in my cock. She didn't fight me because she wanted me to possess her. She wanted me to claim all of her, every single inch of her body.

I couldn't be rough with her, not yet. She was still injured, still recovering. The gauze around her chest had been changed, and now it covered less skin. Her normally flawless body still had faint scars that hadn't faded completely. She was still prohibited from intense exercise, but that didn't mean she could just lay there—and let me have her.

I folded her legs underneath me and positioned my cock against her entrance. The head of my length could feel the moisture ooze from her delectable pussy. I slowly pushed inside then slid as far as her channel would allow me.

She inhaled a deep breath. Then she said my name, packed with uncontrollable passion. "Diesel..."

I sank deep inside her and held myself on top of her, careful not to distribute any weight on her body. Our sex had been restricted to missionary, but I still enjoyed it immensely. As long as I got to have her, I was happy.

Her ankles locked together around my waist, and she tugged on the lace panties that restrained her arms above her head.

"Don't. Move." My hands dug into the sheets on either side of her, and I slowly thrust inside her, feeling her cream sheathe me all the way to my balls. She was full of thick arousal, coating my dick with both her desire and love.

"Yes, Boss Man..."

I never wanted someone to take her away from me again.

I wanted to know she was there—wanted to feel she was there.

Every day for the rest of my life.

"Diesel. That's how you address me." I pressed my mouth to hers and sucked her sexy bottom lip. I'd wanted to be the boss man when she was just a woman I was sleeping with, but now she was so much more. She was the woman I'd committed my life to. I wanted her to call me by my name, a name very few people had the right to address me by.

She kissed me back, her lips trembling. "Diesel…"

I rocked into her a little harder, sometimes kissing her and sometimes breathing with her. My cock fell into her pussy, slathered in her arousal. My soul fell into hers at the same time, my heart growing bigger just for her. I'd never loved anyone the way I loved her. It was bigger than me, bigger than my world. She'd somehow stripped all the essentials away and showed me that money and possessions meant nothing—nothing compared to her.

She was beautiful underneath me, the sexiest woman that had ever had her legs wrapped around my waist. She refrained from moving with me because she was forbidden to, so she let me make love to her. Every time she took my cock, she took a deep breath. Every time I hit her in the right spot, she forgot to breathe altogether.

"I love you..." She breathed into my mouth, her eyes open and looking into mine. Her devotion was the biggest turn-on because she meant it. She wasn't saying the right things to turn me on. Everything that came out of her mouth also came from her heart.

"I love you, baby." I pushed deep inside her before I pulled out again. My hips wanted to buck and I wanted to slam into the headboard with force, but my heart slowed everything down. I could only take her easy, make love to her without moving her at all. The restraint didn't hurt the sex. It enhanced it because it made it more meaningful. I could go downtown and find a woman who would give me wild sex for the night, but that didn't sound the least bit appealing.

It was nothing compared to what I had now.

What I had was perfect.

She came, her thighs squeezing my waist hard. "Diesel...yes." Her cheeks filled with color and her mouth gaped open as the moans poured out. Even if she was dead silent, her pussy expressed her emotions for her. She squeezed me tightly with a grip that rivaled a snake's.

Every time she squeezed my cock like that, I wanted to come.

I wanted to come hard.

She pulled on the panties again.

I growled in her face.

She relaxed again, riding out the rest of the orgasm. Her head rolled back, her nipples hardened, and her moans stretched on for another minute.

I watched her with fascination, feeling more like a man for making my woman come like that.

When she finished, she opened her eyes again, full of pleasure from the satisfaction of that orgasm. "I want your come, Diesel."

"I want to make you come again."

"You will...but I want it first. I want your seed inside me...feels so good."

My spine tightened. All the muscles in my back shifted as they contracted against my bones. Nerves fired off as the words circulated directly in my blood. She was the only woman who had taken my come, and I loved giving it to her.

My pumps continued as my dick hardened. I thickened further, my breaths turning labored with intensity. My hand snaked into her hair, and I secured my grip on her even though she wasn't going anywhere.

"Diesel, give it to me..."

The second I heard those words, I was done. I came inside her, stuffing her with mounds of my arousal. I breathed against her mouth as it all released, filling her tiny pussy. It felt even better every time I did it. "Tatum..."

She softened underneath me as she felt the weight of my come. "I want more."

My come was already seeping out of her entrance and dripping onto the sheets. She couldn't handle the amount I gave her, but she wanted to be stuffed with more—over and over. "Then I'll give you more."

THE CLOCK ON THE WALL SAID IT WAS FOUR A.M.

I was in the living room, sitting in my sweatpants as I stared at the blank TV screen. A scotch was in front of me, and I took a few sips to wash away the nightmare that still burned behind my eyes.

I tried to forget it.

Nightmares didn't happen often for me.

But now they didn't stop.

Tatum never survived in my dreams. She wasn't quick enough to push the gun away, and she bled out on the floor of her lobby. I always stood near the doorway and watched the scene. Not once did I try to help. I stood by and did nothing, not because I was scared, but because I couldn't move.

I didn't save her.

I watched Bruce Carol shoot her in the face. I watched the smoke rise from the hot gun.

And I didn't do a damn thing.

I dragged my hands down my face before I drank my scotch again. The sleep was still behind my eyes, and if I didn't stay awake, I feared I would slip back into the nightmare. I grabbed the remote and turned on the TV. The only entertainment that had no meaning was sports, so I watched a replay of a game that aired earlier that day.

And I kept drinking.

"Diesel?"

I turned to the hallway and saw Tatum standing there in my t-shirt. Her hair was messy from tossing and turning in bed, and her eyes were lidded from interrupted sleep. I'd been sitting there for a while, so she must have woken up when she realized my massive size was no longer acting as her personal heater. There was no hiding the scotch in front of me —or the disturbed look in my eyes.

She walked to the couch as she ran her fingers through her hair, pushing it away from her face so she could get a better look at me. "Everything alright?"

"Yeah...just couldn't sleep."

Her gaze intensified, calling my bluff without saying a single word. She had this natural ability to say her thoughts with just her expression. Her irritation filled the living room, and it continued to build as the silence stretched on.

I gave her the truth since she could see through my bullshit. "Nightmare."

She came around the couch and sat beside me, my shirt still reaching her knees even with her body bent. All of my clothes looked like blankets around her petite frame, but she somehow looked better in them than I ever did. Her hand slid to my thigh, and she gave me a gentle squeeze. "What happened?"

"Don't want to talk about it."

"It might help."

"I don't want to scare you." I didn't want to put these horrific ideas in her head. She was the one who'd actually lived through my nightmare. Why would she want to be reminded of it?

"Nothing scares me, Diesel." She took my hand and rested it on her thigh, our fingers interlocked together.

She was telling the truth. She never showed fear in the face of danger—even when it wasn't smart to do so. "It's about what happened...I keep having the same nightmare over and over. I jerk awake, and then I'm too afraid to go back to sleep."

"Talking about it will help."

I stared at the TV, feeling her powerful gaze on the side of my face. "I can always talk about it with someone else."

"Not if the dream is about me." She commanded me to look at her just with her tone of voice.

I turned my gaze back on her.

"I don't lose sleep over what happened. It came and went...it's over. I don't look over my shoulder in fear. Bruce Carol tried to kill me, but he underestimated me. I shot him in the neck and the face, but the memory doesn't make me shake. He tried to cross me—and he got exactly what he deserved. Life goes on, and I will go on as well. Despite my injuries and my suffering, I'm a very happy woman. I survived the ordeal, and I've been surrounded by the people I love. So you can tell me, Diesel. You can tell me anything."

My eyes softened as I looked at the resilience on her face. She was the kind of light that never burned out. When dusk arrived and the sun was absent, it still shone on—it just couldn't be seen. But with Titan, her light was everywhere. When the sun was gone, her light still reflected in the stars in the dead of night. It was my job to be the stronger partner in our relationship, to guide and protect her. But I found myself humbled by her strength. I found myself looking up to her rather than the other way around. "In my dream, he succeeds. And I'm standing there...doing nothing to stop it." My stagnant position wasn't caused by fear. I stood there because there was nothing else I could do. An invisible force held me back, making me useless in the situation.

I had been useless to her.

She brushed her soft fingers against my knuckles. "We both know what the dream means, Diesel."

It was obvious to me every single time I had the nightmare.

"You aren't responsible, Diesel. Let it go."

"I should have been there..."

"That's not true," she whispered. "I don't need a man to protect me. The only person I need is myself. You're my partner, not my savior. I want to share my life with you, not hand it over to you. You need to forgive yourself."

"I can't..."

"Then I'll make you." The wonderful fire was in her eyes, the flames that drew me to her in the first place.

I remembered the way my father changed after my mother died. It happened so fast that he couldn't process it at the time. He stared at the front door like he kept waiting for her to walk inside. "I know my father relives that day over and over again. If only she hadn't gotten in that car, she'd still be here right now. That's how I feel now. If you hadn't gone home alone...it never would have happened."

"If it didn't happen then, it would have happened some other time. And I'm glad it happened, Diesel."

My eyes narrowed on her face.

"Because now it's over. I survived, and I'm going to make a full recovery. I never have to worry about him hunting me down again. That relief is a wonderful gift. It's much better than the fear of waiting for it to happen. The biggest turmoil of our relationship has come and gone. Enjoy this feeling of freedom. Enjoy this feeling of safety."

I stared at our joined hands, knowing I needed to listen to her. She was the smartest person I knew, so logical that it made me seem irrational. She put everything in perspective so well.

"Forgive yourself, Diesel."

"I need you to forgive me first." I squeezed her hand.

A soft smile came over her lips. "There's nothing to forgive, Diesel. But I'll give it to you...if that's what you need to hear."

I did need to hear it. I needed to know that this was really behind us, that we would move forward and find happiness. "I promise to protect you for as long as I live, Tatum. I know I'm supposed to make that promise on our wedding day...but I'm making it now."

"You don't need to make a promise like that, Diesel. But I accept it anyway. And I give the same promise to you."

She'd been looking out for me since the beginning. She could have taken that deal with my father, but she remained loyal to me. Her loyalty had never faltered since the day we met, even during our worst times. I wasn't just a lucky man because of Tatum's beauty and success. I was lucky because of all the beauty in her heart. She was the greatest person I knew—and she loved me with all her heart.

I was damn lucky.

MY SUIT WAS LAID OUT ON THE BED, AND TATUM HAD a fiery look in her eyes the second I woke up that morning.

I connected the dots quickly.

She wanted me to go back to work.

"Breakfast and coffee are on the table, and your suit has just been pressed. You better hustle." She insisted on doing things for me around the house, like cooking or laundry, because she said she needed stuff to do. Not going to work every day was driving her crazy.

We hadn't revisited this conversation—at least, not formally. Her opinion on the matter was clear, and the longer I stayed home with her, the more aggressive she became.

I was still torn.

Work was piling up the more I stayed out of the office, but I suspected I'd worry about her the entire time I was gone. I was torn between two sides, two desires. I dried my hair with the towel before I tossed it in the laundry basket in the walk-in closet. "Baby, I'm not sure about this."

"You're going." She was in my t-shirt with black leggings, and her hair was already done as well as her makeup. Her energy hadn't returned to normal because she still had tremendous physical weakness. She could move around the house for a few hours before she needed to take a long break. She tried to hide her fatigue from me, but I knew her better than she realized. Weakness was a word that didn't exist in her vocabulary.

"You have a lot of medication to keep track of."

"And I'm smart enough to figure it out. I've been taking it every day."

"What if you—"

"Diesel, I'm fine. You belong at the office. You have so many things to take care of. As much as I love spending the day with you, you have other priorities. If I need something, I won't hesitate to call."

The weeks had stretched by, and I was getting restless at home too. I hadn't been working out either, and I felt the subtle changes in my body. As much as I wanted to be with Titan, my other projects weighed on my mind. She was more than stable, perfectly capable of getting around the penthouse on her own. But I would never stop worrying. "You're sure about this?"

A smile broke on her face, the genuine kind that reached her eyes. "Absolutely. Please go, Diesel."

I stood naked in the bedroom, and it was a testament to her dedication that she didn't stare at my package. Whenever my clothes were gone, sex was always on her mind. "I'll check on you throughout the day. But I want you to call me if anything comes up."

"I know."

"Promise me?" I didn't want her to refrain from calling me just because she was afraid to bother me. Work needed to be taken care of, but its importance still paled in comparison to her.

"I promise."

I wrapped my arms around her waist and pressed my face against hers. There was nothing else in my life that gave me as much meaning as this woman. If I'd lost her, I would have lost everything else too. Happiness hadn't been a regular theme in my life, but now that I had it every single day, I was terrified to lose it. Tatum completed me in a way money and fancy cars never did. "I love you."

She rubbed her nose against mine. "I know you do."

REPORTERS FOLLOWED ME EVERYWHERE I WENT. FROM

the moment I left the penthouse to the instant I stepped inside my building, they pestered me with questions about Tatum's health and our upcoming nuptials.

I ignored them.

Once the elevator doors opened, I walked onto my floor and saw the surprised looks on my assistants' faces.

They obviously hadn't expected me to show up.

I went to Natalie first. "I know I have a lot to catch up on. So let's start now."

"Of course." She grabbed a folder and stuffed a bunch of papers inside. "How's Titan doing?"

"She's recovering. She'll be good as new in no time."

Natalie and I walked into my office and got to work. My meetings had been canceled for the foreseeable future, so we got everything back on the calendar. I had thousands of unread emails, contracts, and updates on my various companies. It would take a month just to catch up on everything.

A few hours later, Jax called my cell.

The last time I saw him, Tatum had been shot. I couldn't even remember what we talked about. I remembered his face, but not a single conversation. I took the call. "Hey." It was awkward to address him because I wasn't used to speaking to my brother.

"Back at work?"

"Yeah...how did you know?"

He chuckled into the phone. "It's all over the news, man."

I rolled my eyes, annoyed that my life was more important than the serious shit going on in the world. "Tatum pressured me. She said it was time I moved on."

"Doesn't surprise me. She doesn't strike me as the kind of woman that needs to be taken care of."

"No, she's definitely not." She liked to solve her own problems. She preferred to take care of herself before she let anyone help her. It wasn't a matter of pride, but of strength. She let me in more than anyone else, but even then, she could be difficult.

"I wanted to see if you wanted to get lunch. We haven't talked much..."

We hadn't talked at all. I'd greeted him at dinner, but we hadn't said much. In the back of my mind, I thought about the work that had piled up in my absence. I should attend to it before I ventured into my social life. But this was my brother, and he should have priority. "I don't think it's smart for me to leave the office when every reporter in Manhattan is following me. How about we meet here? One of my assistants will grab something for us."

"That works for me. What time?"

I looked at my watch on my wrist. "How about shortly after one?"

"I'll see you then."

JAX WALKED INTO MY OFFICE IN A CRISP SUIT AND TIE. Black on black, he looked like a darker version of me. We had the same jaw, the same eyes, and our builds were similar to our father's. There was no doubt we were related—and we were definitely brothers.

He approached my desk with his hand in his pockets. A slight smile was on his lips, but the rest of his facial features were hard. "I'd shake your hand, but that feels strange."

"Yeah, you're right."

"But I think it would be weirder if we hugged."

"True."

"And we aren't doing that stupid fist-bump thing either."

"Nope."

"So I'm just going to sit." He fell into the armchair in front of my desk.

"Works for me." My assistant had picked up salads and smoothies from one of my favorite places down the street. Jax was built the same way I was, so I could only assume he watched what he ate and hit the gym with the same dedication. I handed over the food, and we ate in our comfortable positions.

"How's Titan?" Jax asked. "From what Dad has told me, she's doing really well."

"She is. She's up and about, but she still has a lot of pain. We have a few more doctor's appointments and treatments to do before she's fully recovered."

"Physical therapy?"

"No. Her limbs weren't compromised."

"That's good." He stabbed his fork into his salad and ate slowly, focusing on the conversation more than eating. "Dad said he's never heard of someone recovering from a tragedy so well. He says it's like she wasn't shot at all..."

"She's definitely a fighter." No matter what the obstacle was, she conquered it. She could achieve anything she put her mind to because she didn't accept defeat. I should have known that bullet wouldn't kill her—because she wouldn't allow it to.

"It's not the time for me to be proud of her...but I am."

"And that badass woman is going to be my sister-in-law...pretty damn cool." The second he mentioned our familial bond, things became tense. We hadn't said more than a few words to each other in a decade. We'd lost so much time over something so stupid. My mother wouldn't be happy about it if she knew.

I sipped my drink and avoided his gaze for a moment, feeling the awkwardness intensify. A silent conversation passed between us, but we knew it couldn't stay silent much longer. It had to be addressed eventually. I didn't blame Jax for what happened. He seemed to be stuck in the middle of it all. But the outcome of the war still ripped us apart.

He addressed it first. "I'm not sure where to begin..."

"It doesn't matter where we start. We're going to end at the same place."

He placed his salad on the table beside him. "I never disliked Brett—"

"I know you didn't." Jax didn't have hateful feelings toward anyone. He'd never been that way.

"I saw the things Dad did to him, but I never interfered. Then when you walked away, I didn't know what to do. I'd always been close with Dad, and we were already doing business together. No matter what side I picked, I knew I would lose. I never anticipated it becoming a decade of war..."

"I didn't either."

"I'm sorry about a lot of things." One ankle was positioned on the opposite knee, and he rested both arms on the armrests. His cuff links were visible, metal squares that reflected the light from the ceiling. He hadn't shaved in a while, so a full beard covered the bottom portion of his face. He was two years younger than me, so we were both over thirty. But in my eyes, I always saw him as my younger brother—one who was naïve and innocent. "I'm sorry I didn't stand beside Brett when I should have. I'm sorry I cut you out of my life just because Dad did. I'm sorry I let so much time pass."

"You don't need to apologize to me, Jax. I'm sorry too."

"I do," he said quietly. "I should have done the right thing."

"The right thing wasn't so simple. Brett is your family, but so is Dad. It was a complicated situation. I don't hold it against you."

He stared at me with a similar expression to my own. We looked so much alike, it was like staring at a mirror. His emotions were easy to read because I made the exact same expressions. "Why are you being so easy on me? We both know I don't deserve it."

Maybe I was being easy on him. I was harsh with my father because I expected more from my hero. But I viewed Jax in a completely different light. When I looked at him, I thought of our practice in little league. I thought about the dinosaur toys we would share. I thought about hooking up with girls from different schools at parties we didn't belong at. "Because you're my brother."

12

THORN

AFTER I HUGGED TITAN, I looked around the penthouse. There wasn't a big, territorial man there, the guy who had resembled a bear more than a human lately. "Where's Diesel?"

"At work." She was in leggings and a loose sweater. When she walked to the bar and made me a drink, her movements were a little more graceful. Her strength was increasing every single time I saw her. She made me an Old Fashioned before she set it on the coffee table and took a seat. "Which makes me happy."

I sat beside her and drank from the glass. "Thanks for the drink, but you don't have to make me anything."

"We always drink together when you're over here. Why would that change?"

"Because you aren't drinking." I leaned back against the couch and rested my arm over the back.

"Well, I would be if I could…it'll be a while before I'm allowed the luxury of alcohol."

"Then I won't either." I pushed the glass away.

"Then what are we supposed to drink together?" she asked with a laugh. "Water?"

I grinned. "Yeah…that doesn't seem like us."

She got comfortable in the chair, her skin full of color unlike it was before. "So, what's going on at Illuminance?"

As a friend, I would normally tell her about all the dirty shit I did with Autumn. When I shared my stories, it was never in a bragging manner, just a friend talking to another friend. She didn't refrain from telling me about her sexual conquests either. I knew Diesel in a way he didn't even realize.

But I didn't mention anything to her. Something kept my mouth shut. I didn't know what it was. If Autumn and Titan were going to work together, it seemed like a conflict of interest to share the details of my bedroom adventure. It might make Titan view her differently, and that wasn't fair. So I bottled it up inside like a gentleman, even though I didn't want to. "Everything is going well. Nothing for you to be concerned about.

You keep everything so organized that it hasn't been difficult to jump in."

"Thanks. I'm relieved it's going so well. It's unfortunate that things didn't work with Ms. Alexander. You're sure you can't change her mind?"

No doubt in my mind that I couldn't. "I actually wanted to talk to you about that."

"I'm listening." Titan adopted her serious mood anytime business was on the table. Even in her relaxed attire, she looked like she belonged in a conference room.

"Ms. Alexander isn't going to change her mind. She has a very interesting character. But you can't afford to have her as a competitor. With any other person, I'd say you could destroy them. But since she's the source of innovation, it's a different scenario. She has a brilliant mind, and you aren't going to recruit a scientist of her caliber. I say you revisit the idea of a partnership. I think it could only benefit you, Titan. And rejecting her offer could only hurt you. That's my take on it."

She stared at me with that icy expression, absorbing the ghosts of my words as they drifted across the room. Her brilliant mind was working furiously, dissecting my words with invisible knives. The longer she stared, the more I feared she knew about my fondness for Autumn. I suspected she was about to accuse me of it right then and there. Thankfully, she didn't. "I'm surprised you feel that way."

"It's the only solution. The only thing stopping you is your pride."

"I don't work well with other people."

"I realize that. But you'll have to make an exception if this is a path you want to follow. You've already accomplished so much that you could abandon this and still retain your professional power. But if you pursue it, you could be securing one of the greatest innovations the world has ever seen. Wouldn't you rather share that responsibility with someone than lose it altogether?"

Her piercing gaze turned more forceful. "I've never heard you speak so highly of someone, Thorn. You speak of Ms. Alexander like she's made a significant impact on you."

Her impact was more than significant. "I've met a lot of people in this business, and most of them are full of bullshit. They've been handed their wealth from their families, and they're as stupid as an ox. But Ms. Alexander is just like you. She pursued her dreams in a storage shed until they came true. She doesn't have just the intellect you need, but the ambition and drive. You two are a lot alike—in many ways."

"That's not necessarily a good thing..."

"In this case, I think it is. You should take this compromise, Titan. You'll regret it more if you don't."

She finally turned away, her lips pursed as she considered it.

I waited for her to make her decision. Titan considered propositions from every single angle. She anticipated the least likely events so she was prepared for anything. After a few minutes, she returned to the conversation. "I trust you, Thorn. So I'll give it a shot."

I smiled in response, glad she was on board. "Great. I'll speak to her."

"But I want to speak to her myself. Can you have her come here so we can speak face-to-face?"

I saw an issue with that. "What about Diesel?"

"What about him?" she countered.

"I thought you weren't supposed to be working."

She rolled her eyes. "It's just one meeting. He'll get over it."

"Do you not know Diesel?" I asked incredulously.

"Well, I'll make him get over it. Did you talk to

Vincent about Kyle and me doing business with him?"

I let her change the subject. "Yeah, he mentioned it. I'm meeting Kyle tomorrow."

"Great. You really are on top of things."

"Of course. Your best interests have always been my best interests."

She smiled at me. "You've always been so good to me. I hope one day I can reciprocate."

She'd given me more than she realized. Just having a loyal friend in this cruel world was more than enough. "You already have, Titan."

Nearly a week had come and gone since I'd last seen Autumn.

We had a great night together, and she slipped out the following morning before I woke up—the second time.

After one-night stands, I usually forgot about the woman and moved on with my life. They were moments that only existed at that particular instant in time. Once it was completed, it was just a memory I could barely recall.

But I hadn't stopped thinking about her.

Her kiss.

Her touch.

Her perfect pussy.

She was a lay I wouldn't forget—not anytime soon.

I knew she wouldn't forget about me either. She was the recipient of a long night of pleasure. I fulfilled fantasies she didn't even realize she had. She begged me to fuck her because I was so good at it. She'd wanted my big cock from the moment she laid eyes on it, and her expectations were never let down.

I gave it to her good.

Whether she was thinking about me or not, she didn't contact me.

I wasn't sure if I expected her to or not.

Maybe I did. Maybe I didn't.

After I spoke to Titan, I knew it was time for me to seal the deal with Autumn. I purposely waited a few extra days so our last interaction would feel fainter. When I walked into her office, I wanted it to be about business. I didn't want her to think I was making some kind of move on her.

After I had my appointment scheduled, I went to her facility on the other side of town and waited in the lobby. It looked exactly the same as before, sleek and simple. I was offered water and a pastry, but I declined both.

The glass walls of her office were completely blacked out so I couldn't see a thing.

But she could see me.

Was she looking at me right at that very moment?

I hoped I could keep my dick under control because she had no problem staring at it. It was a declaration of my innate attraction to her. Now that I'd had her, it was difficult for me to view her as just a potential business partner. Now I thought of her in dirty scenarios, of the way she said my name when my dick was buried inside her.

I couldn't think about that right now.

Her assistant led me inside, and I walked into the large room with the desk near the back. Her long hair was pulled back, and she wore high-rise jeans with a blouse. She was dressed far more casually than usual, so I assumed she'd been doing lab work rather than business at her desk. "Hello, Thorn. How are you?"

I stopped in front of her desk and didn't shake her hand. She never extended the greeting, so I didn't either. Despite our attempts at being professional, there was no denying our last interaction.

Could we really shake hands after the passionate night we'd had together? It seemed beneath us at that point. "Good. You?"

"I'm great."

I eyed one table near the opposite wall, which was scattered with papers and tools. "Long day?"

"Just working on a few things. I had a few issues, but that's what my life is...trial and error."

I sat down and crossed my legs. "Working on anything interesting?"

All she did was smile and sit down. "I'm assuming your visit means Titan had a change of heart?"

So she didn't think I was there for any other reason. That was good. "She has. She's given it some consideration and thinks working with someone with your strengths will only benefit her."

Now the smile she wore seemed genuine. "That's great news. I'm very happy to hear that."

"Titan is looking forward to your collaboration."

"When she's back on her feet, right?" she asked. "I can wait until she's well again."

"Actually, she wanted to know how you would feel about meeting in her home. She would like to meet you in person. She knows you by reputation, but not by introduction."

"I would love to. Just let me know when and where." With the same sultry voice she used before, she commanded my respect so easily. But the tone reminded me of the way she begged me to fuck her, the way she dug her nails deep into my back.

I stopped breathing for a moment, treasuring the memory. Of course, my dick swelled to life when I wished it wouldn't, but just the sound of her voice turned me on. I liked her casual outfit and the way her hair was pulled back. Something about seeing her work was a turn-on too. I guess I liked a strong woman who called the shots.

That was strange because I liked to be the one in charge.

Now that the business conversation was over, there was nothing left for me to do. All I did was stare at her.

She stared back.

I didn't want to stand because she was bound to notice the hard rod in my slacks.

Dammit.

"I'll set it up with her. She lives pretty close to my place." Autumn knew exactly where I lived because it's where we'd hooked up. It was the closest I'd ever gotten to mentioning the actual event we were both thinking about.

"Great. Will you be there?"

"Yeah. I'll be part of the conversation."

"Great."

Now the silence was back, her wordless dismissal evident. She obviously had things to do. So did I.

But I didn't want to stand.

My jacket was buttoned in the front, but that wouldn't hide all of it. The shaft was so thick it was incredibly noticeable. Normally, I wouldn't care if a woman saw how hard I was, but I didn't want to extend an invitation.

Our hookup was over.

I rose to my feet. "Thank you for your time. My assistant will call you." I turned my body slightly, casually hiding my front so she wouldn't have a clear view of my package.

She walked around the table, her heels clicking against the hardwood floor. Her fingers dragged across the desk as she made her way to my side. I could walk away, but her presence commanded my stillness. She stopped directly in front of me and looked up into my face.

Those plump lips. Those bright eyes. Those high cheekbones. Those freckles on her cheeks.

Fuck, I was a goner.

She had so much power over me—and I liked it.

I loved her confidence because it didn't cross into arrogance. I loved the way she owned the room, even if I stood in it. I loved the way her eyelashes were so thick.

This woman was more than most men could handle.

Not me.

Her fingers pressed against my chest, her finger-tips stroking down my silk tie. Her perfume smelled of vanilla and summer flowers. She watched her fingers caress me before she looked up into my face again.

Sexy.

"Come over tonight." She didn't ask. She only told.

I thought that was even sexier.

But I wasn't looking for a relationship, even with a gorgeous woman like her. I'd love to fuck her a few more times, but if it led to a conversation about commitment, I wasn't interested. "I'm not looking for anything serious. The other night was supposed to be a one-time thing. I'm sorry if you misunderstood."

Instead of softening her eyes in heartbreak or narrowing them in rage, she pressed her lips tightly together as she tried to suppress a laugh. She dragged her hand down my chest until she pulled it away entirely. "Wow, you're arrogant."

"Arrogant? I just want my intentions to be clear so you aren't disappointed."

This time, she really did laugh.

My eyes narrowed.

"Thorn, there's only one thing I want from you. The second I saw your toolbar, I wanted to see you use it. You exceeded my expectations beautifully, and it's nice to be with a man who can make my toes curl. A lot of men say they have the same talent, but that's all bullshit. You, on the other hand, are not bullshit."

Now I felt like an idiot for spitting out those words. I wished I could take them back and shove them back down my throat.

"A relationship is the very last thing I want from *you*." She turned away, brushing her hair behind her shoulder. She sat down behind her desk and didn't look at me again. "You should get going. I have a lot of things to do."

She dismissed me coldly, obviously not interested in having me over anymore.

I fucking blew it.

I DIDN'T KNOW WHAT POSSESSED ME TO ACT LIKE SUCH an idiot.

Why did I even say that to her?

She didn't ask me out to dinner.

She invited me to her apartment. That was it.

It was obvious she just wanted a hookup.

So why did I sabotage it by acting like an asshole?

Now I was alone in my penthouse, watching TV and drinking scotch. I could be fucking a gorgeous woman, pleasing her from head to toe, but I was sitting there drowning in my liquor. When I was at the office, I considered retracting my statement and making a move.

But I'd already done enough damage.

Now I pondered what to do. I didn't have her number because I'd never asked for it. The best solution was to find her on social media and send her a message, but that would just come off creepy.

I didn't do creepy.

I could go out and pick up someone else, but I didn't want to do that either.

There was only one woman I wanted to spend the night with.

And if I couldn't have her, I didn't want anyone else.

I SAT AT TITAN'S DESK WITH THE PHONE PRESSED TO my ear. I was on hold, waiting for Autumn's assistant to put me through to her. I wondered if she would know the real reason why I was calling. It'd only been a day, and that was too soon to coordinate a meeting with Titan.

She was a smart woman. She probably knew exactly why I was calling.

Autumn's hypnotic voice came over the line. "Hello, Thorn. Have you scheduled a meeting?"

Hadn't even considered it. "No."

She turned quiet, letting the silence envelop me.

I embraced it.

If she wanted to get rid of me, she would have just hung up on me. But she stayed on the line, which gave me some power.

She still wanted to fuck me. "I spent the night with you last night."

She knew exactly what I meant. "I hope it was as good as last time."

"Not quite. Did I spend the night with you?"

She chuckled. "That arrogance again..."

"Am I wrong?"

She never answered. "What do you want, Thorn?"

"You."

"I picked up on that."

"Now look who's arrogant," I countered, a smile stretching across my face. "Come over tonight."

"I'll think about it."

My grin widened. "That's a yes, isn't it?"

"It's a probably."

Now that I was about to have her again, my hands shook in anticipation. I wanted to grip her firm tits and flick her nipples with my thumb. I wanted to taste the valley between her breasts. I wanted to suck that bottom lip into my mouth until it was swollen. I wanted to taste her luscious pussy again and listen to her beg me to fuck her. "I'll see you then."

"Goodbye, Thorn."

"Goodbye, Autumn."

She arrived at my penthouse at eight.

It was late, so she obviously wasn't expecting dinner or wine. She walked into my living room in heels and a raincoat. She hung her purse by the door and slowly peeled her jacket away, revealing nothing but a black thong and matching bra.

She didn't waste time.

My eyes were glued to her gorgeous body as I walked toward her, my eyes drowning in her endless curves. Her piercing in her navel was undeniably sexy. The way she stripped her coat away and stared at me with such confidence made my cock press harder into my sweatpants. I was shirtless and barefoot, and now my sweatpants felt constricting against my raging cock.

My desire couldn't be bridled, and my hand immediately shot into her hair so I could jerk her head back. I directed her face toward mine, and she immediately moved with the motion instead of fighting it. My mouth found hers, and I kissed her just the way I wanted. I let my mouth explore hers, let my tongue penetrate her mouth. I felt her own greet mine, and together, they danced erotically.

My fingers dug into her luscious ass, and I pulled her tight against my cock.

She moaned when she felt him against her stomach.

I kissed her harder, our embrace turning passionate almost immediately. Not a word had been exchanged between us, but there wasn't any need for small talk. She was only there for one reason—to fuck me.

My hand tightened on her hair, and my fingers snaked down the front of her panties. I found her clit and immediately circled it with two fingers. I rubbed it harder, making her breaths shorten.

Our mouths opened and closed, our kiss continuing right in my doorway. The sexiest woman in the world had just walked into my penthouse like she owned it. She stood in black lingerie, hardening my cock the second she was in my vicinity. She had iron-clad control over my dick, making it hard on command.

I rubbed her clit harder.

She breathed deeper.

She had a lot of control over me, but I had just as much power over her.

My fingers slid back to her entrance, and I fingered her while my thumb circled her clit. "So fucking wet for me." I spoke against her mouth before I continued to kiss her.

Her hand dug down into the front of my pants, and she gripped my hard dick with her warm hand. "So damn hard for me."

I tensed at her touch, relishing the softness of her hands. When she started to pump me, I breathed harder, loving the way she pleasured my dick so effortlessly. I continued to finger her and rub her clit at the same time.

We were both so hard up we were about to come right in the middle of my living room.

"Thorn..." She gripped my shoulder for balance, her fingers cutting into me. "I'm about to come."

"I know." I kissed her as I stared into her eyes, perfectly aware of the way her pussy was tightening around my fingers.

"I want your big dick inside me."

"Don't worry, you'll get it." I ended our kiss and peered down into her face. "But you're going to come now." I wanted her to understand she was at my mercy, that I had the power to make her feel anything that I chose. She could walk in the door then be climaxing two minutes later. I didn't just have a big dick—I had a lot of other things.

She hooked her arm around my neck and stopped fighting the explosion between her legs. She looked into my eyes with her scorching ones, the cosmic ball of fire burning everything in my living room. She came around my fingers, tight and dripping. She ground her clit against my thumb, getting off to it even harder.

I enjoyed the show, my dick throbbing in her hand.

She bit her bottom lip before she released a powerful moan. Her breathing turned to quiet screams. Her nails nearly drew blood as she clung to me desperately. As the climax passed, she started to loosen her grip on me, her nails no longer cutting into me. The look she wore made my cock thicken even more because she wasn't wearing her tough expression anymore. Her hardness had been stripped away, and now just the woman remained behind. She was real, vulnerable, and gorgeous.

I kissed the corner of her mouth. "Now I'll give you my cock—and make you come again."

———

HER HAIR WAS IN DISARRAY, HER LIPS WERE SWOLLEN, and her makeup was slightly smeared. She lay beside me in the dark, the sheets and comforter kicked to the foot of the bed. She was turned on her side, so the prominent dip in her waist was noticeable. She was either tired from the hour or tired from the sex—maybe both.

My fingers started at her knee then slowly slid to her hips. I felt her softness, which was similar to touching a rose petal. Her toned legs were sexy, and the tightness of her waist from her abdominals was sexy too.

She was perfect.

My hand snaked over her hip until I reached the dip in her waist. My hand slid under her arm, and my thumb brushed over her ribs until I palmed one tit. Her body was mesmerizing. I'd been with a lot of women, controlled most of them, but none of them possessed her fine elegance. No matter what her position was, she had the firmest tits. Her olive skin was delicious. I'd already explored her body, but I wanted to taste her more. I wanted her to stay exactly like this. "You're a very beautiful woman." I lay beside her on the same pillow and hiked her leg around my waist. I'd already taken her so many times, but my cock was hardening all over again.

Her mouth didn't smile, but her eyes did. "Thank you." Her fingers explored the hardness of my chest and stomach. Her fingers traced the lines and grooves, feeling every inch of my visible strength. Sometimes she looked down at my skin, and sometimes she looked into my eyes. "You're a pretty man."

"Pretty?" I asked.

She chuckled. "Sexy man. Is that better?"

"Much."

She pulled her hand away then peeked at the clock on my nightstand over my shoulder. "It's getting late. I should get going..." She turned over and slid to the edge of the bed.

We'd gotten down to business without exchanging a single sentence. Now she didn't try to spend the night or make small talk. She got what she wanted, and she was leaving without a backward glance.

I'd slept around a lot, and one-night stands were a major part of my resume. But while women claimed that was all they wanted, they always wanted more. They just took their time getting to the point.

But that didn't seem to be the case with Autumn.

She really wanted nothing from me.

A woman as beautiful and successful as she could have any guy she wanted. She probably got tired of all the offers and didn't want anything at all. Maybe that was why she was attracted to me— because I was the first man not to throw myself at her. My indifference was transparent. I made my cold intentions clear, and that was a relief to her.

I got out of bed and pulled on my sweatpants.

"You don't have to walk me to the elevator." She walked out of my bedroom naked, her gorgeous ass shifting from left to right as she moved. She had the perfect hourglass figure, a woman so sexy she looked like a walking sculpture.

I forgot to speak because I was staring at her so hard.

My dick hardened too.

I followed her into the living room and watched her pick up her thong from the ground and her bra from the couch. "I don't mind."

She pulled her black thong up her long legs then straightened the lace over her hips.

I stared, watching how naturally sexy she was. She wasn't even trying to catch my attention, but she did it so effortlessly.

Her bra came next, the straps secure over her shoulders.

How could I fuck this woman so many times but still want her? "So, how is this going to work?"

"How is what going to work?" She didn't look at me as she prepared herself for the outside world. She slipped her heels on her feet then grabbed her rain jacket off the ground.

"This." I crossed my arms over my chest as I stood in front of the elevator.

She pulled the jacket around her body then

straightened the collar as she looked into my eyes. "I wasn't aware there was a *this* to discuss."

The corner of my mouth rose in a smile, finding her cold attitude hot. "What is this?"

She tied the belt around her waist, securing the jacket around her petite body. "I thought we established this was meaningless fun? Let's keep it that way. You made it clear you don't want anything more. Neither do I."

"But we both want to do it again."

Her eyes narrowed slightly, a confession of agreement. She slid her hands into the pockets of her jacket as she looked at me.

"And again. So, am I free to text you?"

She considered it while pressing her lips together tightly. Even when she was deep in thought, she looked provocative. I couldn't imagine what it would be like to work with her every day, to stare at her beautiful features and do nothing about it. "Yes. But that's the only thing I want to hear from you."

"Trust me, I'm not going to ask about work." Our pending collaboration was the last thing on my mind.

"And strict professionalism when we're working together."

I smiled. "Agreed."

She turned to the elevator and hit the button so the doors would happen.

Before she could step inside, I grabbed her by the elbow and yanked her toward me. I wanted to feel those plumps lips against my mouth one more time. I wanted to feel her breath fill my lungs. I wanted to feel the way she trembled slightly when she was the recipient of my passion.

She kissed me back the instant she felt me. Her fingertips moved up my chest until she reached my shoulders. She gave me her tongue when I didn't give her mine. She sucked my bottom lip and matched my aggression. She'd just been trying to leave, but now she got me fired up the same way she had when she first arrived.

She was the first one to break away.

I knew I wouldn't have.

"Goodnight, Thorn." She pushed her hand against my chest as she turned away.

I almost snatched her again. "Goodnight, Autumn."

She stepped into the elevator and leaned against the back wall as she waited for the doors to close. Her eyes were on me, her look as intense as mine. If she didn't have such restraint, she'd walk back in here and ride my dick again. I'd never been with a woman who got so wet for me. She kept up an act of indifference, but there was no denying how much she wanted me. Her pussy betrayed her in the most obvious way possible.

The doors finally began to close.

My arms rested by my sides as I watched them come together. My eyes remained focused on hers until she was finally gone from my sight.

When the elevator descended, I suddenly felt the emptiness of my penthouse. I wished I were walking back to my bed to find her sleeping underneath my sheets. She'd be there for me when I woke up in the morning.

And I could fuck her before I went to work.

13

VINCENT

"It's nice to see you back at work." I stepped inside my son's office, seeing him returned to normalcy in his navy blue suit. He no longer wore the sorrow that had tainted his features from the moment he heard Titan had been shot. That fear had finally passed, and like after a long winter, the color was finally returning to his cheeks.

"It's nice to be here, partially."

I sat in the chair facing his desk and stared at my son, a man who looked so similar to me it was unsettling. Sometimes I thought of him as a boy, but when he was just as tall as I was and built like a mountain, I couldn't view him as anything other than a man. "I'm guessing Titan is behind this?"

"She pushed me out the front door."

I chuckled. "She's right, though. Life goes on."

"I still worry about her. I check on her a few times a day. But she's always doing well."

"There's nothing you can help her with at this point," I said. "Now she needs to wait to heal. Unfortunately, that takes time. When you've been shot in the chest, the wound doesn't just disappear overnight."

"I know. I'm looking forward to her being well again. Even though the doctors say she'll be fine, I won't drop my guard until it's officially over."

"Understandable."

Diesel sat back in the leather chair and looked at me. A moment of silence passed between us, a quiet conversation that lacked words. We'd spent so many years apart that it was still strange that we were back together. It was the nicest feeling in the world to just sit with my son...to be welcome in his presence. "Jax told me he stopped by."

"Yeah, we had lunch."

"He said you were very forgiving."

Diesel broke eye contact, probably because he knew he was much harsher with me than he was with Jax. "He's my brother. It's hard for me to stay angry with my brother. I knew he was stuck in a difficult position. He either lost his father or lost his brothers. In either scenario, he lost."

I nodded. "I'm glad you see it that way."

"I would try to spend more time with him, but right now, everything is so hectic."

"It is," I said in agreement.

"I really don't know anything about him anymore. All I know is stuff I read in the headlines, but there's no way to know if any of that is true."

There were a lot of things going on in Jax's life, things he wasn't ready to share yet in light of Titan's shooting. It would have to wait until a better time. "He's not much different. Still the same little shit he's always been."

Diesel chuckled, showing his handsome smile he inherited from me. "You're probably right. How are things with Brett?"

"Better. I've been meaning to ask him to do something. I've just been busy..." I thought about my lunch meeting with Scarlet Blackwood. She was surprisingly easy to talk to for a woman who existed in a world where only appearances mattered. She was understanding, attentive, and interesting.

"Busy with what?" Diesel cocked his head to the side, seemingly interested in my response.

"I'm doing a piece with *Platform*. They have a new line of suits they want me to model."

"That's a big deal. They're huge."

"Yeah. I also did an interview."

Diesel shook his head. "Interviews are the worst. I don't do them anymore."

"I didn't mind this one."

"That's cool. Does that mean you're going to the Designer Guild's anniversary party tomorrow, then?"

There were so many functions going on in the city that it never seemed to stop. Any reason to have a party was a good enough reason. It made the lines between work and social life blur. Sometimes they were one and the same. "Yeah. Connor is getting an award and asked me to go."

The mention of Connor immediately soured his look. His eyes narrowed, and the smile he once wore was now gone. The only reason I noticed those subtle clues was because I was his father. He'd had the same reactions since he was a child. Some things never changed. "Are you bringing anyone?"

"No." I'd probably run into an old flame there, but I did my best to end relationships positively. I made my intentions very clear in the beginning, that I wanted to someone to spoil for a short period of time. I warned them not to get attached to me because I wasn't worth their investment. They would marry someone else someday. I was just a stepping stone, an experience so they would understand what they really wanted in a man in the long term.

Diesel didn't press me on the topic. Tatum had asked me about my personal life before and was pushing me in the direction of a meaningful relationship. I never told her I had an open mind about it. No matter how old Diesel was, it would be strange for him to see me with a woman that wasn't his mother.

It was strange just to think about my being with someone besides his mother.

"Is there anything I can do to help?" My son was a man and didn't need me for anything anymore. But I would always be his father, so I would always ask. He would say no every single time, but maybe one day he would say yes.

"No. But thanks."

"I'm guessing you won't be attending the party?"

He shook his head. "I'm not going anywhere unless Titan is on my arm. Spending the night pretending to care about fashion and social elites sounds painfully boring. Not sure how you stand it."

"I just have more patience than you," I teased.

"I don't believe that," he said. "I get my stubbornness from you."

"You get a lot of things from me, actually." The

very reason he was sitting on the top floor of this building was because he'd looked up to me his entire life. I had been hard on him since he started to walk. I taught him the real meaning of manhood. He would pass those lessons on to his own son, and the Hunt tradition would continue.

"Yeah, I suppose." His eyes shifted away from my face. "Thanks for stopping by. I should get back to work."

I took his dismissal in stride. I rose to my feet and buttoned the front of my suit. "I'll stop by in a few days to see Tatum."

"She'd like that." Diesel walked me to the door. "And have fun tomorrow night. Let me know how the article turns out."

"I will." I'd missed out on a decade of hugs from my son, so I hugged him now.

He reciprocated and patted me on the back. "See you later, Dad."

I would never get tired of hearing my children call me that. From the first time I'd heard it, it felt special to me. "See you later, son."

I ARRIVED IN MY BULLET, AND THE VALET TOOK MY

car. Cameras were immediately in my face, the various flashes no longer affecting me because I was used to the annoyance. A reporter stuck out her microphone and blurted out a question about Tatum.

I ignored her and walked inside.

It was nice not having a date because I didn't have to drag her through this bullshit.

I made it inside the old opera theater and saw the stage lit up for the show. Models in their finest dresses passed me as they rushed off to talk to someone. Most of them were in dazzling gowns with endless glitter. Heavy makeup was on their faces, so when they weren't under the stage lights, it didn't look quite right.

I made my way to the reception room and was immediately offered a drink.

I skipped the champagne and went straight for the scotch, not interested in bubbly drinks in pretty glasses.

I saw a few friendly faces and mingled.

Thirty minutes later, I spotted Alessia across the room. Judging by her eyelash extensions, voluminous hair, and the dark eye shadow that was painted across her lids, she was one of the models for the evening. With classic Italian looks and untouchable beauty, she stared at me with the same devastated expression she gave me the night I broke it off.

I didn't want to ignore her. I could do the awkward thing and pretend I didn't see her, even though we both knew I saw her. But that wasn't my style. I finished my glass and set it on an empty tray before I walked up to her. She was in a ruby red gown covered with diamonds that made the dress worth tens of thousands of dollars. It was perfect to complement her Tuscan skin and dark hair. "Alessia, you look lovely." My arm circled her waist, and I leaned in to kiss her on the cheek.

"Thank you..." She let me kiss her before she pulled away, still wearing the same forlorn expression. For a woman so beautiful, she shouldn't be sad over a man like me. Right now, she didn't see it, but moving on from me was the best thing for her. She should be with a young man, someone still excited about life. She shouldn't be with a man who was over thirty years older than her. At least, she shouldn't have gotten so attached to me. She shouldn't have fallen in love with me—especially when I told her not to.

"This dress fits you perfectly."

"I know. Connor is a genius. He understands my body better than I do."

But not better than me. "You're going to outshine everyone tonight."

She smiled slightly and looked away. "Still charming, huh?"

"I mean it."

She chuckled, but in a cold way. "Have you been taking this as hard as I have?"

I didn't answer because the truth would make me an asshole. Her company was pleasurable, and I enjoyed our adventures on my yacht and through the countryside. But her presence was just a way to pass the time. She made me laugh, made me smile, gave me good sex when the sun was down, but that was the extent of her purpose. "It's never easy for a man to let such a beautiful woman go." I didn't want to hurt her, ruin her. She had a long life ahead of her, and when she found the man she wanted to spend that life with, she would understand the love she had for me would never compare. I would be nothing next to her husband, just a memory she hardly recalled. I knew that from experience... because meeting Isabella completely changed my life.

"I know you told me how it would be. I know of all the women before me...all the women after me. But young men aren't like you, Vincent. You're so mature, gentle, sophisticated...I miss you." She peered at me through her thick eyelashes, her bright blue eyes gorgeous. "I miss what we had...our friendship."

"I miss it too, Alessia. I enjoyed your company a great deal."

"Then why did you leave?" Music played overhead, so her words weren't audible to those around us. We could have a private conversation even in a room full of people.

Alessia was one of the women who didn't seem obsessed with my money. She was easy to talk to and asked about my sons a lot. But she did seem smitten with my power, the invisible protection I wrapped around her. Standing in my shadow made her feel more powerful. She felt safe with me, looking up to me almost as a father figure. She had a difficult time growing up because her family was poor, and there were a lot of bumps in the road. With me, she knew she had a man who would take care of her. "It had nothing to do with you, Alessia. I know you're sad right now, but trust me, you deserve someone better than me."

"There is no one better than you, Vincent. You're the kindest man I've ever known." Her hand moved to my forearm. "You're such a gentle giant. They don't make them like you anymore."

"When you meet a nice man your age, you'll feel differently." She wanted a family and a fulfilling life. That was something I would never compromise on. I already had my children, and they were grown men now. I didn't want to start all over again, taking care of a baby in diapers. I already had a legacy to carry on my name. "But you know I'm always here for you. If you ever need anything at all, all you have to do is call." I leaned into her again and kissed her on the cheek, bringing a sense of finality to the conversation. It almost felt idiotic having this conversation when Alessia was such a beautiful woman. She was pouring her heart out to me when I was far beneath her. I might have money, but I didn't have her elemental goodness. She was soft like silk, easy to the touch. I was hard and callused, far too broken for someone so innately good. "Good luck tonight. I know you'll do wonderfully." I dropped my hand and immediately stepped away, knowing I had to put space between us. I didn't want to upset her before her performance. Perhaps seeing her wasn't the best idea.

I grabbed another drink and swallowed half of it in a single gulp. The fire seared my throat all the way down to my belly, and it ignited me with a warmth that was intensely soothing. When I looked across the room, my eyes fell on Ms. Alexander. The last time I saw her, Thorn had been in deep conversation with her. I wondered if their words had amounted to anything—or they just burned out.

I kept walking until my eyes spotted a brunette I thought I recognized. In a bright red dress with only one sleeve stood a woman I'd seen not too long ago. Around the waist, the dress was missing cuts of fabric, showing her bare skin. The dress fit snugly around her wide hips and down her thighs and hinted at her abs through the fabric. It stopped above her knee, and black stilettos were on her feet. She held a black clutch embedded with diamonds.

It was a classy look.

She fit right in with everyone else.

Her brown hair was loose that night, trailing to her shoulders. It was straight and shiny. Her makeup was heavier than it'd been the other day, and now she looked like one of the models about to hit the runway. The only difference between her and the girls was her age. It was noticeable in some places, but in every other way, she could compete with the girls on the stage. She had the perfect size and grace.

It made me wonder if she used to be a model in her prime.

She was speaking to a woman who appeared to be the same age. They exchanged a few more sentences before the woman was pulled away by someone else.

Scarlet turned her gaze on me. A slight flash of recognition came into her eyes. Her pupils dilated before they relaxed again. Then she gave me a smile that was completely different from the one she'd just been wearing.

Now it looked real.

I crossed the room then stopped in front of her. "Ms. Blackwood, how are you?" I liked her name. It was filled with such historical reference and power. It was heavy with elegance too, the kind of poise that she carried. My hand moved to her hip, and I leaned in and kissed her on the cheek.

A thrill immediately went down my spine at the contact. I didn't touch her that way when we met last week, but at a function like this, it was the cordial way of doing things. I just didn't expect to enjoy kissing her—or how natural it felt.

She didn't flinch at my touch, and her smile widened. "I'm well. How are you?"

I was doing a lot better now that I was talking to her. "Good. Can I get you a drink?"

"No, thank you. I've had way too many already." She was standing in front of a framed image of *Platform* magazine. It was protected behind glass with an art light pointed directly at it. A famous actress was on the cover.

I nodded to the wall. "Looks nice."

"Yes, that was a special edition." She turned to examine the cover with me. "And she's very sweet. I think people find her intimidating because of her beauty, but she's very down-to-earth."

Instead of looking at the picture, I stared at Scarlet instead. I watched the way her face lit up with a smile as she stared proudly at her work. In the short amount of time I'd spent with her, it became apparent how much she loved her work. It wasn't just a job to her, but her entire life. "Can I ask you something?"

She pivoted her body back to me. "Considering the way I interrogated you last week, I think that would be okay."

"Have you modeled?"

Instead of just smiling, a blush filled her cheeks. "You flatter me, Mr. Hunt."

Employees and acquaintances called me that. It

didn't feel right hearing her address me so formally. We were surrounded by alcohol, half-naked women, and loud music. This wasn't a business meeting. "Please call me Vincent."

"Very well. Then you must call me Scarlet."

"I will."

"To answer your question, yes. I did a very long time ago. That was how I got started in the business. I modeled evening gowns and lingerie. When I retired from that career, I still wanted to be involved in fashion and beauty. That's how I got here."

The idea of her modeling lingerie got my attention. "How long ago was that?"

"I retired when I turned thirty. That was twelve years ago."

She was forty-two. She was fourteen years younger than me. That didn't seem like such a big difference when most of my companions were in their early twenties. "What do you love more? Modeling or running the magazine?"

"I don't love one more than the other. They're completely different. I had a very illustrious modeling career, and it gave me such an adventurous life. But once it was time to close that chapter, I wasn't too upset about it. It was time to move on.

Now I'm in a different chapter of my life, and I've embraced it."

I liked her perspective on life. "That's a good way to look at it."

"Thirty is very old for a model, as young as that seems. I could have continued, but it would have required cosmetic surgery, and that was a route I didn't want to take. It looks great on some women, but I knew it wasn't for me. Aging is nothing to be ashamed of, and I feel just as beautiful now as I did then."

"I agree with you." It was one of the things I'd first noticed about her. She had hints of age, but that didn't deter from her beauty. She was definitely gorgeous, and her natural looks highlighted her features even more. She reminded me of myself, embracing age while taking care of her appearance as much as possible—naturally. I'd been with models for a long time, but I found Scarlet far more beautiful than all of them. I couldn't explain why.

"I just don't think a woman should change her appearance to be considered beautiful."

"You're right. And you don't need it, Scarlet."

The blush filled her cheeks again. "You're very sweet, Vincent. I understand why the girls adore you."

"The girls?" I wasn't sure to whom she was referring. I'd seen in the tabloids that the media considered me to be a very sexy man despite the slight gray that had come into my hair. They said I'd aged phenomenally well, and people couldn't believe my age when I said it. But I didn't have fangirls the way a boy band did.

"The models," she explained. "Meredith, Natalie, Alessia...you've been mentioned quite a few times."

I supposed it was naïve to think they didn't talk about me when I wasn't around. I never spoke of them to anyone because it wasn't the gentlemanly thing to do. And it must be awkward between them, knowing they all dated the same man.

"Don't worry, they only said good things."

I always treated them like goddesses, so I hoped they didn't have any ill feelings toward me. If I ever ran into any of them, I would always stop and say hello. "That's good to know."

"Alessia seemed to take the breakup hard. She's been eating even less than usual."

"I'm sorry to hear that." I didn't want any woman to be sad over me. I wasn't worth their time, not when there was something so much better out there.

Despite the heavy subject, her opinion of me

didn't seem to change. "Have models always been your type?"

"I suppose." I didn't plan for it on purpose. It just seemed to happen that way. Whenever I met them at a social event, I recognized them. We started talking, and one thing led to another.

"Was your wife a model?"

I didn't talk about Isabella. I'd already made that clear. "Is this off the record?"

"Vincent, nothing is on the record unless you want it to be. And I know you don't want this printed."

She could be leading me into a trap, but she didn't seem like that kind of person. Instinctively, I felt like I could tell her things I couldn't share with others. She seemed understanding, compassionate. "Yes. We met when I was in college. I told her I wanted to take care of her, so she quit modeling so we could have a family."

"You must have been young at the time."

"Very. I was twenty when I met her."

"I had my daughter at the same age. It must have been love at first sight for you."

"No." I stared at the picture on the wall, thinking of the first time I laid eyes on her at a party off campus. "It was more than that." Isabella had looked at me, a smile on her lips. I had no idea how I'd looked when I stared at her. In that moment, I somehow knew that beautiful brunette was destined to fill my heart for the rest of my life.

Scarlet's eyes softened, filled with emotion. "You had Diesel when you were twenty-one?"

"Yeah."

"Then she must have had Brett..."

I didn't like talking about it. "Yeah, she was very young."

"And her being a young mother didn't bother you?"

"No." Ordinarily, I wouldn't have been interested in a woman like that. But Isabella was different.

"So then you must have gotten married almost immediately after you met."

"Yeah. I asked her to marry me six months after I met her."

Scarlet seemed genuinely interested in what I was saying. It didn't seem like she was asking out of politeness. "Wow, then your relationship must have been intense."

"It was." I asked Isabella to marry me, took care of her while I finished college so she could raise our family, and when I launched my first company and became a millionaire, I bought her a small apartment in the city. As my wealth grew, I lavished her with more things. We had Jax shortly afterward, and then our family was complete.

"I'm sorry about what happened," she whispered. "I know it doesn't mean much, especially since she's been gone for so long, but I mean it."

"Thank you, Scarlet." As the years passed, some things got easier. But I never stopped missing Isabella. I never stopped dreaming of her. Some days were better than others. Some days, I could think of her fondly and appreciate the memories I had of her. But other days, it was difficult just to get out of bed.

I noticed Scarlet didn't wear a wedding ring, but that didn't necessarily mean she wasn't married. "Do you have someone in your life?"

"No. I've been divorced for almost ten years now."

"I'm sorry."

"Oh, don't be," she said with a scoff. "I shouldn't have married him in the first place. I was young when I had Lizzie, and getting married seemed like the right thing to do at the time. But we did it for the wrong reasons, and it wasn't a good relationship."

"Your daughter's name is Lizzie?" I asked.

"Yeah. She's a sweet girl."

"Do you have a picture of her?"

"Of course." She smiled brightly as she pulled out her phone. Her wallpaper was a picture of her daughter, a young brunette that looked just like her. She had a nice smile, the same colored eyes, and she had the appearance of a kind person. "She's at NYU right now. She wants to be a nurse."

"That's nice."

She put her phone back in her clutch.

"She's a beautiful girl."

"Thank you. I'll never say this to her, but having her was the most difficult thing I've ever done. It was twenty at the time and getting started with modeling. Money was always difficult, and my husband wasn't a good man. But she's the most important thing in my life, and she's my whole world. I couldn't imagine my life without her. She completes me more than any relationship I've ever had."

That was exactly how I felt about my sons. The fact that I could still see Isabella when I looked at them made me cherish them even more. "I think that's how every parent feels about their kids." I noticed it was the second time she'd spoken ill of her ex-husband, and she unleashed a harsh insult. "Your ex-husband wasn't a good man?"

Her gaze shifted away, and her smile died. "Yeah, but that doesn't matter anymore. It's in the past—

where it belongs. My daughter keeps in touch with him, but she doesn't have a clue what happened between the two of us—and that's how I want it to be. I don't want Lizzie to hate her father—even if she should."

Now I wanted to know more. Did he hurt her? Did he break her heart? I shouldn't care about something that happened over a decade ago, but I did care. She dismissed the topic with her last statement, so I didn't press the subject. But that didn't mean I wasn't still curious. "She's your only child?"

"Yep. So she's a bit spoiled." Her smile returned when the subject of her ex had been dropped. "I've never known a love the way you describe with your wife. In my experience, men aren't heroic or romantic. Maybe it's just the line of business I'm in, but the handsome men I encounter are either jerks or gay." She chuckled at the end, laughing it off. "Or just mostly gay."

A woman across the room called her over. "Scarlet, let me introduce you to Tom!"

Scarlet waved back before she turned back to me. "Excuse me, Vincent. I hope you have a good night. I'll let you know when I'm finished with the article." She gave me a smile before she turned away.

I wanted to grab her, but I didn't. "Scarlet."

"Yes?" She turned back to me, her acquaintances staring at us from their formation.

I didn't know why I asked her to turn around. I guess I didn't want her to walk away—not yet. Our conversation was intriguing, and I found myself wanting it to continue. She wasn't exceptional, but I found her interesting. I loved the way she smiled so genuinely, the way she adored her daughter and wore her heart on her sleeve. I loved the way she still held herself so elegantly even when the subject turned heavy. "Have lunch with me tomorrow."

Her smile fell as a blank look entered her expression. She obviously hadn't been expecting me to make that request.

In all honesty, I hadn't been expecting to do it.

But I knew I wanted to keep talking to her—and not in a crowded room where people could distract us.

I wanted it to be just the two of us.

I wanted to look at her beautiful face and watch her stare back at me. I wanted to know everything about her life, everything about her daughter. I wanted to see her in tight clothing, see the way her waist still curved in so sexily. She didn't look like a forty-two-year-old mother exactly the way I didn't look like a fifty-six-year-old man.

I'd been with the most beautiful models in the world.

But they didn't hold a candle to Scarlet Blackwood.

She was more than a pretty face.

She was a pretty soul—a soul that had pierced through my armor and touched mine.

Finally, she answered, "I'd love to."

I ROSE FROM MY CHAIR WHEN SHE REACHED THE TABLE, and I greeted her with a kiss on the cheek just as I did last night.

She leaned into it, expecting it this time.

I pulled out the chair for her then sat down.

She did the same.

She wore a black blouse with large shiny buttons down the front and a tropical blue scarf. Her hair was in curls that day, and the strands floating around her shoulders. She was in black jeans, and the dark colors made her look even thinner than she did last night. She wore a few rings, rose gold and sparkly.

I realized I hadn't said anything to her yet. "Thanks for meeting me."

"Happy to be here." She smiled at me, immediately bringing a sense of comfort to the table. "I don't think I've ever seen you dressed in anything but a suit before."

Since it was Saturday, I was in dark jeans and a long-sleeved black t-shirt. The bulk of my wardrobe consisted of suits because that's what I wore most of the time. It was nice to wear something casual on the weekends. A lot more comfortable than the thick material that had been measured to fit my frame perfectly. It was always constricting, no matter how soft the fabric was.

"You look nice," she added.

"Thanks. You look nice as well."

She smiled then looked down at her menu.

The waiter came over and took our drink orders. Since we were ready, we made our entrée selections too. We were sitting right against the window, people passing back and forth outside on the sidewalk.

"Did you stay late last night?" I'd met up with some acquaintances, and we'd watched the fashion show from one of the closer rows. I connected with Connor Suede later, and he introduced me to Ms. Alexander. She was a highly intelligent scientist who had changed the entire landscape of energy. Then Thorn stepped into the conversation. It seemed tense at the time, but I wasn't sure if that was real or just my overactive intuition.

"Later than I wanted to. But I did have fun. What about you?"

"I left shortly after the show. After I had a few words with Connor, I left."

"He's a fascinating man. He really has a talent when it comes to fashion. It's truly incredible. I bought a few of his jackets years ago, and I still wear them regularly. To him, the fabric is more important than the design. His simple approach to wardrobe is what I like the most. Sometimes you see designers debut these loud outfits that just don't seem practical."

I nodded in agreement even though I couldn't relate. The same woman had been picking out my clothes for years. She knew what I liked and what I despised. Fashion had never been important to me —only money.

She looked down and chuckled. "I'm sorry. I could ramble on about fashion forever…"

"No need to apologize. You know what you love."

"And what do you love, Vincent?"

I led a very simple life despite my wealth. There were only a few things I cared about. "My sons. I'm very lucky that they've transitioned from sons to friends. I love sports. I love to golf. My favorite hobby is to sail through the Mediterranean on my yacht. An excellent wine paired with the right cheese is something I look forward to every time I'm in the South of France. And once in a while, I allow myself the luxury of freshly baked bread."

She hung on my every word, like she was imagining all the sights in my mind.

"Those are the things I'm passionate about."

"I liked how you didn't mention work at all."

I didn't realize that until now. "I've accomplished everything I've wanted to do in the business world. I'm proud of my achievements, but I'm no longer passionate about it. There's more to life than work."

"Well said. It sounds like you do an excellent job of balancing work and pleasure."

"I work hard so I can play hard." Alessia and I took a trip to Greece together just a few months ago. We explored Santorini from my yacht, and I fed her grapes while she lay around in her bikini. Those quiet moments of beauty wouldn't be possible if I didn't hustle at the office.

She nodded. "Well said again."

"Have you traveled much?"

"I've been to Italy and France many times for work. In fact, I'm there regularly. Both are beautiful countries. I love every moment when I'm there. I haven't sailed in a yacht, but the view from land is still wonderful."

"Have you taken your daughter along?"

"No. She's very involved in her own life. She's always wanted to be a nurse, so she's volunteered at the hospital for a long time. And now that she's in school, she's very committed to her profession."

"She's ambitious."

"Very." Like always, she smiled when she spoke of her daughter.

I rested my back against the chair and kept my shoulders straight. My eyes were glued to her face, and I couldn't help but stare. My gaze was naturally intimidating because direct eye contact didn't unnerve me. But when it came to some people, I had to be careful.

With Scarlet, she didn't seem to mind. Sometimes she held my gaze, and sometimes she looked away.

Nothing else in the restaurant took my notice. I was more interested in the freckles on her right cheek and the thickness of her eyelashes. She wore a dark lipstick, and that made her smile more apparent.

And more beautiful.

"I spoke to Alessia at the end of the night."

I already knew where this was going before she even finished.

"She mentioned you."

I held her gaze, unsure what to say in response. My conversation with Alessia didn't go poorly, but it didn't go well either. "She's a nice woman. She'll bounce back."

"She had a lot of nice things to say about you. She said you're the most wonderful man she's ever met...and she loves you."

I didn't want Alessia to love me, not when I didn't love her in return. I wanted her to find happiness in a man much better than me. "I never meant to hurt her. I told her up front what our relationship was. Maybe I let it go on too long. Maybe I should have warned her better. I care about her and don't want her to be in pain. I wish there were something I could do, but there's nothing I can do."

When Scarlet mentioned Alessia, there didn't seem to be any accusation in her tone. She seemed to be asking as a friend rather than a nosy person. "When you date women like Alessia...what exactly are you looking for?"

Our relationship had shifted from professional to something else. Now we seemed to be friends, exchanging stories about life. There wasn't judgment on the table. There was only understanding. "Companionship."

"And nothing more?"

I shook my head. "Nothing more. Alessia deserves to be with a man who can give her everything she deserves. I'm not that man. She wants a family someday, which is something I'm not interested in. She's looking for passionate love, and I can't offer her that either. The only thing I can offer is exotic trips, expensive jewelry, and good sex." It didn't seem appropriate to talk about such crass things so bluntly, but that was the entire truth.

"Do they usually want more?"

"Sometimes. I suspect some of them think they can change my mind."

"Change your mind about what?" she asked.

"About something more serious."

"Is there a reason why you aren't looking for something more serious?"

Now I knew we weren't talking about the article at all anymore. This was just between her and me. "When I lost Isabella, all of my love was buried with her. I couldn't imagine loving someone, not after I loved her. So I decided to have short-term relationships that would give me what I needed."

She nodded slightly, as if she understood.

"What about you?" I wanted to know what she was looking for. I wanted to know what she wanted in a man, in a partner.

"What about me?" she asked.

"What's your romantic life like?"

"Pretty boring, honestly," she said with a chuckle. "I haven't been on a date in...at least a year."

A year? That was a long time to go without some kind of companionship. I was single for three years after Isabella passed away. That's how long it took me before I could begin to feel attracted to other women. I didn't want to say something rude, but silence was worse. "That's a long time..."

"Yeah, it is," she said with a sigh. "But most of the men my age are happily married. So the dating pool is pretty small. And the rest of the men usually consist of weirdos or jerks. I don't want to settle for someone I'm not truly in love with, so I'd rather be alone. And being alone isn't all that bad. My sister lives here, so I see her all the time, along with my nephews. And I have my daughter, of course. I have great friends and a wonderful job. I don't need a man to complete me. At least, just any man..."

I understood her perspective. I hadn't tried dating anyone my own age because I wasn't looking to get remarried, so I went after women who were too young for me. This was the first time I'd sat across someone who was actually compatible with me.

That scared me a little bit.

Silence stretched between us, growing heavier by the second. I noticed the necklace around her throat and the subtle eye shadow on her lids. There was a single freckle at the top of her wrist. The longer I was in her presence, the more I absorbed her into my memory. It was difficult for me to imagine a woman like her ever finding a man good enough for her. It didn't surprise me that dating was virtually impossible.

The waiter brought our food, shattering our silence momentarily.

Now that we grabbed our silverware and ate, the quiet wasn't as noticeable. I knew our lack of conversation wasn't due to discomfort. In fact, it was the contrary. We didn't need to fill the silence with words to make it easier.

I liked that.

I was a man of very few words. I liked a woman who accepted that, who didn't ask if there was something wrong just because I had nothing to say.

She took a few bites of her salad then stared at me across the table. "Any news on Titan?"

"She's the same." Sitting at home and waiting for the healing process to finish.

"Do they have any wedding plans?"

"Not that I know of. I suspect they'll tie the knot the second she's better. Neither one of them wants a big wedding."

"A big wedding isn't necessarily a better wedding."

"I thought about offering Isabella's dress to Titan, but I'm not sure if I will."

Her eyes softened. "You still have it?"

"It's in my closet." I'd packed up most of her things and put them in storage. It was too difficult to throw her things away, like her favorite cardigan or the scarf she always wore around Christmastime. But I didn't want to see them every single day either. Her dress was one thing that I kept. My collared shirts and slacks all hung in a row. At the very end was her white dress in the plastic covering.

"I'm sure Titan would feel honored if you offered."

"But I already gave Diesel her engagement ring. I think I should save the dress for the next son who gets married...to make it fair."

"Aww...Titan is wearing her ring?"

I nodded.

"That's very sweet."

It'd been sitting in my nightstand ever since I buried Isabella. My ring was with hers. It took me two years after her death to finally stop wearing it. "It looks great on Titan. I think Isabella would be happy to see her wear it."

"Too bad they didn't get to meet."

Too bad she didn't get to experience so much with me. She died far too young. I would always be bitter about it. I was supposed to go first. "Yeah. But I'm sure she's watching over us. She's seen the fine men the boys turned out to be. She's seen all my mistakes as well as my redemption."

"And I'm sure she's very proud of you too."

There was nothing to be proud of, if you asked me.

As if she could read my mind, she responded to my thought. "You raised those boys on your own. They all turned out great, so you must have done something right. You carried on even when it was difficult. Not many people would have been as strong as you."

"You're too kind." The only thing that kept me going was my boys. If I hadn't had them, I wasn't sure how I would have made it through that difficult time. Even today, they acted as my crutch.

"I'm being sincere, Vincent. You shouldn't be too hard on yourself."

"Even after what I did to Brett?"

She shook her head. "Everyone behaves differently when it comes to grief. You can't judge someone when you've never known that kind of pain. Loss turns you into a different person. It affects each of us differently, just as medication affects everyone else differently. You really shouldn't be so hard on yourself. I know your wife wouldn't want you to."

"You think so?" I whispered.

"I know so."

"How?" I'd always wanted Isabella's approval, but I wouldn't get it until my time had come.

"Because she loved you."

14

THORN

I TALKED with a few people and made my appearance at the fashion party. As time went on and I was in the public eye more, fewer people saw me as the man who was engaged to Tatum Titan—and then dumped by Tatum Titan.

People were starting to see me as Thorn Cutler again—just a man.

I had a few drinks, shared a few laughs, and then spotted Vincent Hunt across the room. He wore a midnight black suit with a matching tie. Thick like a bull, he stood out against the crowd.

And Autumn was with him.

I didn't know what the two had in common, but judging by the fact that Connor Suede was standing with them, he must be the missing piece. Vincent had done some modeling for Connor, and so had I. Maybe Autumn did too.

My eyes grazed over her body, seeing the luscious curves in the champagne pink dress she wore. It was an exceptional color on her slightly darker skin. Against her black hair, the color popped even more.

I set my drink aside and joined their conversation, my eyes trained on Autumn.

Vincent noticed me first. "How are you, Thorn?" He shook my hand.

"I'm well. You?"

"Great." He gave me a polite smile before he turned to Connor. "Connor was just telling us about a new line of shoes he's been working on."

"Thorn Cutler." Connor shook my hand. "A man who always looks good in a suit."

I nodded. "Nice to see you again." Before I had a chance to greet Autumn, Connor took the lead.

He wrapped his arm around her waist and looked down at her, more than just professional affection in his eyes. "Let me introduce you to my next star, Autumn Alexander."

She smiled up at him, obviously comfortable with the way he touched her.

My smile disappeared.

"Ms. Alexander is going to be wearing some pieces for me," Connor continued. "I know she'll add a spark to every photograph." He was dressed in a gray V-neck sweater with black slacks. He had a tight and rigid body, and he had good looks that could get him out of any kind of trouble.

I didn't like him.

Titan told me details about her physical encounters with him. He was an intense man, and he knew how to handle a woman in the bedroom. She'd been attracted to his confidence and his skill.

I really didn't like him.

"Autumn and I are well acquainted." I wasn't thinking clearly because my temper had been ignited. The possessive way he handled her dug deep under my skin. He was staking a claim right in front of me. He was a flirtatious man because he worked with women all the time. He knew he was handsome, rich, and talented. My arm circled her waist, forced his to move, and I pulled her into my side for a one-armed hug. "We're going to be working together very soon."

Autumn maintained her composure, but she flashed a slightly alarmed look in my direction.

"You are?" Vincent didn't hide his surprise,

knowing I was covering Titan's businesses in addition to my own.

"Yes, Titan as well. It'll be a great partnership." I should drop my arm from her waist because the physical contact shouldn't linger for so long, but I wanted that asshole to keep his hands off her. Before this incident, I'd liked Connor. But now I despised him for some reason.

Autumn gently stepped away from my embrace, doing her best to make it seem like the gesture was only affection between two friends. She continued to wear a composed smile while holding her gorgeous body with perfect grace. "Yes. I'm looking forward to it as well."

Connor turned his gaze back on her, his eyes intense. They were heavy and dark, like a storm of clouds was building on the surface. He wore that expression all the time, but it seemed particularly focused on her in that moment.

Maybe I was just being paranoid, but it seemed like he wanted to fuck her as much as I did.

Not gonna happen.

"I've designed these special dresses that will look perfect on Autumn." Connor addressed us, but he held her gaze like she was the only one in the room.

"The curves of her body are more beautiful than lines of poetry. I work with models every single day, and she has a special quality they lack. From the thickness of her eyelashes to the slenderness of her neck, she's more perfect than the wonders of the world."

I wanted to snatch Vincent's drink out of his hand and slam it down onto Connor's skull. Who the hell talked like that? He should do Shakespeare in the Park if he wanted to woo a woman like that. It wouldn't work on someone like her.

But Autumn smiled...and it seemed genuine.

Jesus.

Connor still hadn't taken his eyes off her, having a silent conversation with her.

Fuck, this was bad.

Connor's arm moved toward her waist again. "Sweetheart, let me introduce you to some people we'll be working with..."

I knew that was bullshit. He just wanted to get her away from me.

If I did nothing, she might go home with him tonight.

I shouldn't care if she went home with anyone. It's not like we were exclusive. It's not like I cared about her. I just didn't want to share her with anyone else. This wasn't about romantic feelings, but about male possessiveness.

She didn't mean a damn thing to me.

But I still couldn't let her slip out of my fingers and into his arms. "Autumn, I need to talk to you for a second."

When she turned my way, she didn't hide her surprise. "Right now? Can't it wait?"

I eyed Connor's hungry expression and turned back to her. "No." I grabbed her by the elbow and directed her away from Vincent and Connor. Her skin was warm to the touch, soft like I remembered it. I'd just had her the other night, but it seemed like a lifetime ago. Now that there was another man who wanted her, I couldn't get her fast enough.

I guided her out of sight; that way Connor couldn't look at her anymore.

"What is it, Thorn?" Autumn blurted out the question, her voice full of annoyance.

We stood in a corner next to a blown-up image of *Platform* magazine. An art light shone directly on the glass, and people talked in groups as music played overhead.

"Connor is a great designer, but he sleeps around a lot."

She stared at me blankly, like I hadn't finished my sentence. "Your point...?"

"It's obvious he wants to fuck you."

Her eyes narrowed even more as she tilted her head to the side. She stared at me harder. "And so what if he does? Last time I checked, he's not a married man."

I wanted to stop this from happening without getting my hands dirty, but it didn't seem like Autumn cared about any of those things. "I just want you to understand what you're getting yourself into. If you think working with him is just going to be professional, you're mistaken."

"Nothing is completely professional," she countered. "Look at us. You pulled me from a conversation to tell me something I already know. I didn't get this far in life being clueless. I know when a man admires me for my brain and my body."

"And we both know why Connor admires you."

Her gaze became more hostile. "If we're done with this ridiculous conversation, I'm going to go on with my evening."

"Not even close to being done."

She crossed her arms over her chest, her anger starting to simmer. "Thorn, what's the problem?"

I stared her down without knowing what to say. I

didn't even understand why I'd pulled her all the way over there to speak in private. "I don't want you to fuck him."

Her anger immediately disappeared, genuine shock coming into her features. "Who said I was going to?"

"Are you saying you aren't?"

"What I'm saying is, whether I want to fuck him or not, it's none of your business. I'm free to screw whoever I want—when I want. We agreed that *this* isn't a thing. It's just...there."

"I'm not disagreeing with that. But I don't want you to go home with him tonight. I want you to go home with me, alright?" I felt like a moron saying that to her. I'd never said that to anyone else. All the other women I spent my time with were just arrangements. The parameters of our relationship were laid out in the beginning. Autumn was different because it was completely spontaneous. She came on to me, and I couldn't refuse her.

"Why?"

"Why what?"

"Why do you want me to go home with you tonight?" she asked. "Is it just so I won't go home with him? Or is it because you want me to be with you?"

"Does it matter?"

"You bet your ass, it does. Which is it?"

I slid my hands into the pockets of my slacks, feeling her piercing gaze heavy on my face.

She kept up her stare.

"Both. There's something I want to talk to you about...in private."

"When I said I wasn't looking for a relationship, I meant it."

"I did too." She was getting the wrong impression. "It's something else."

She didn't give me an answer, but her gaze was still tentative.

"Go to my place when you leave. I'll be waiting for you." My natural impulse was to lean in and kiss her, right on the corner of her mouth. It was difficult for me to be in a public setting with her and not touch her in some way. I wanted to extend the pleasures of our relationship outside the confines of our privacy. When she looked so beautiful in that dress and those heels, it was hard to keep my mouth off her skin. I stepped closer to her until our faces were almost touching. "Autumn?"

She quickly stepped back, keeping our interaction professional. "I'll see you there." She walked off without another word, her heels echoing against the hardwood floor.

I watched her go, my eyes following her until she was out of sight.

THE ELEVATOR DOORS OPENED, AND AUTUMN STEPPED inside my penthouse. Her curves were sexy in the tight dress, and her dark hair was in curls. She set her clutch on the table near the entryway then stepped farther into my home.

I left my scotch on the coffee table and rose to my feet, drinking in her beauty in a whole new light. She'd never looked more beautiful as when I couldn't have her. When I stared at her across the room and watched Connor touch her like he had every right to do whatever he wanted, it pissed me off.

Because she was mine.

I crossed the distance between us, feeling her large eyes home in on my face. She held my look with the same confidence, her shoulders back and her chest out.

I moved into her body and wrapped my arms around her petite waist. My mouth immediately descended and I kissed her, kissed her the way I'd wanted all night. I dug my hand deep into her hair, and I yanked on it gently just to feel that she was real.

She kissed me back, like she'd been looking forward to my kiss. She devoured me with the same enthusiasm, her hands sliding up my bare chest until she reached my strong shoulders. She'd been pissed at me earlier, but now that I was caressing her with my kisses, it was like that anger had never arisen in the first place.

She came here to talk, but that impending conversation didn't seem important anymore. My goal was to get her here and away from Connor. Now her body was wrapped in my arms, and she was sticking her tongue down my throat.

Mission accomplished.

We didn't make it to the bedroom and settled for the couch. Her dress was yanked up to her waist, her heels were kicked across the room, and then she was on her back, pressed into the corner of my couch.

I fucked her into that corner, giving it to her harder than I ever had before.

She yanked me into her like I wasn't going fast enough, and the climaxes squeezed my dick until it was bruised. Sweat glistened across my skin, but the heat and fatigue didn't deter me. I was buried between her legs, exactly where I wanted to be. It felt so good, so tight and wet.

I loved fucking her.

When I finally came, I filled so much of the condom I was afraid it would rip. This woman got my engine revving in special ways. She heightened my senses, made me combust with lust. I sucked her bottom lip into my mouth, tasting her sweat and mine, before I pulled out and rolled the condom off in the bathroom.

I wiped the sweat from my forehead with a towel then stared at myself in the mirror. My hair was messy from the way her fingers had run through it, and there was a thin film of sweat over my chest. Subtle marks from the tips of her heels had left indentations in my skin.

I knew I was a lucky man.

I didn't have everything—but now I had her.

I walked back into the living room, and she had already composed herself. Her dress was down, her heels were back on, and her hair had been fixed with her fingertips. Like she hadn't just been fucked on my couch, she sat with her legs crossed and her back perfectly straight.

Made me want to fuck her again.

I sat beside her, my hand moving to her thigh. I squeezed her gently. "I enjoyed that."

"Me too." Her gaze moved to my blank TV before she slowly turned her gaze back on me.

"I doubt you would have enjoyed Connor so much." No man could fuck her as well as I could. Not only did I have the right tools, but I also had the right engine. She was guaranteed a good time when I was in between her legs. I could make her feel fuller than any other man could.

The corner of her lips rose in a smile. "Wow… you're so jealous."

"Not jealous."

She scoffed. "If that's not jealous, I don't know what is."

My fingers tightened on her thigh. "Were you going to go home with him?"

"I don't see why I have to answer you."

"Is that a yes?" I pressed.

She continued to smile. "I'll never tell."

I pulled my hand away, feeling another wave of nausea rush through me. Just picturing her with him made me sick. Anytime I fantasized about her, her legs were spread for only one person—me.

"What did you want to talk about?" she asked.

"Because I hope our conversation about Connor is over."

"I guess I wanted to clarify a few things."

"Alright." She uncrossed her legs and turned her gaze on me.

"I'm not looking for a relationship, and I never will. But I don't want to share you with anyone either. It's not about love, just possessiveness. I don't want you screwing other men when I can give you exactly what you're looking for. We both know you aren't going to find someone who can fuck you as good as I can."

"You aren't arrogant at all..."

"Tell me I'm wrong."

She smiled.

I leaned closer to her, my hand moving to the back of her neck under her hair. "Tell me."

Her smile faded away, and the resignation moved into her expression. She knew she couldn't deny what I said—not when it was true. "You aren't wrong."

Hearing the words from her red lips sent a thrill down my spine. My fingers dug into her hair even though she'd just fixed it, and I kissed her again. Our wet mouths moved together, and our tongues quickly melded into one. The kiss escalated at an alarming rate, and the passion made it seem like we hadn't just fucked on that couch five minutes ago.

I ended the kiss, knowing I had power over her. Like butter, she melted quickly for me. I could make her turn into a puddle right on the couch. Her body came to life for me just the way mine did for her. There was a connection between us—a white-hot one.

My fingers continued to rest in her hair as I stared at her, seeing the sex-crazed look still heavy in her eyes. "You said you weren't looking for a relationship. Is that for the foreseeable future?"

"It's for a while, at least."

"Why is that?" She was younger than me, that much was obvious. She still had time to find someone and settle down. Maybe she was just taking her time.

"Does it matter?"

I saw the walls rise in her eyes. Whatever this was about, she didn't want to share it with me. "No... I guess it doesn't."

"Why aren't you looking for a relationship?"

I held her gaze and only gave her silence.

"Looks like neither one of us wants to talk about it..." She turned into my hand and kissed the side of my palm. Her thick lips pressed against my warm skin, leaving a slight residue from her lipstick. "Then let's leave it that way."

I wanted to know more about her without giving anything in return. But that wouldn't be fair. "What do you want from me?"

"Good sex and convenience. That's all."

"I can give that to you. Wherever you are, whatever time it is, I can give you a lay you'll never forget. I can fulfill any fantasy you want. I can make you stretch like every woman should. I can make you tremble, make you forget the shit going on outside these four walls."

Her eyes remained glued to mine, her intensity mirroring mine.

"So, you don't need Connor. You don't need anyone else but me."

She tilted her head slightly to the side, her lips slightly parted so her teeth were visible. She wasn't doing it intentionally, but she made herself look like the sexiest woman in the world. She could pull it off so effortlessly.

"But I want it to be just the two of us. Do you agree?"

She took her time before she responded, letting the quiet stretch between us. "Yes."

She was officially mine—exactly the way I wanted her. "There's something else I want."

"Alright."

"When I'm with a woman, I like to be in control. I like to be the alpha, to order her to do things that I like. When I command her to get on her knees, she obeys. When I tell her not to come until I say so, she listens. That's what I want from you."

It was the first time the pleasure disappeared from her face. "Thorn, if you're talking about *Fifty Shades* stuff, I'm not into that. I'm not gonna let you hang me from the ceiling so you can whip me. I'm surprised you would even bother asking."

"That's not what I'm asking. All I want is to call the shots—and you listen."

"How is that different?"

"Because there are no chains or whips. There is no pain. But you yield all power to me when we're fucking. I promise you, I'll give you even better sex than you realized was possible. It's what we've already been doing, but better."

After my clarification, her eyes relaxed and the hostility faded from them. "I've never done anything like this before."

"You won't regret it."

She turned her gaze away, her expression one of concentration as she thought to herself.

"Tell me what you're thinking."

She pressed her lips together briefly before she opened them again. "I'm a very busy woman, and taking the time to meet someone new and be disappointed is frustrating. A lot of men act like they know what they're doing, but when it comes down to it, they don't know how to please a woman. With you...you're very talented." She looked into my eyes without shame for what she said, and there was no reason to be ashamed. "You've got a very nice package, and you know exactly what to do with it. That's the kind of man I'm looking for...one who knows how to fuck. So it sounds like the perfect arrangement for me. I don't see a downside."

"Neither do I." Every time she flattered my cock, my ego inflated. There was nothing better than hearing a beautiful woman compliment my dick like that. She was transparent in her thoughts, telling me exactly what she was thinking.

That was sexy.

"Then we have an understanding," I said. "You give me your tests, and I give you mine." Not only did I want to keep Connor away from her beautiful pussy, but I wanted to be inside her—skin-to-skin. I wanted to feel her intimately, to feel her lubrication right against my dick. The only way we could do that was through monogamy. Keeping my dick in my pants around other women should be simple since she was the only woman I wanted anyway—for the time being.

"That sounds like a good idea."

When I first saw Autumn, I didn't think there was a chance in hell I could be with her. She was either tied down with someone else, or she wanted a happily ever after. I never expected her to be as detached as I was, to want something meaningless for a long period of time.

It was almost too good to be true.

"Then I should get going." She rose to her feet, walking in her heels to the elevator.

I didn't try to get her to stay. I already got what I wanted, so I didn't want to push my luck. My hands moved around her waist, and I held her in the doorway, looking down at her gorgeous features and pretty eyes. My hands squeezed her waist before I reached a hand behind her and hit the button. My actions were smooth as I kept my eyes glued to hers. "I'm yours. Use me however you want." I kissed her softly on the mouth, pressing my lips against her plump ones. I kept my mouth closed because parting my lips would only ignite the fire of passion once more.

She pulled away, her hands moving down my chest. "I will." She stared at me with the same fiery expression, her nails digging into the skin of my abs. "And just so you know…" Her eyes trailed down my body, taking in my chiseled grooves with obvious obsession. "I was never going to go home with Connor."

My cock came to life in my sweatpants. It was the quickest I'd ever gotten hard in my life.

She leaned into me and pressed a kiss to the corner of my mouth before she turned and stepped into the open doorway. "I only wanted to go home with you." A mischievous smile was on her lips as the doors slowly slid shut in front of her. She kept up the expression until the doors closed fully and she was gone from my sight.

As if I'd been punched in the face, I was glued to the spot. The wind had been knocked out of me, and now I could hardly breathe. One of the sexiest women I'd ever seen just teased me with only her words.

And now I wanted her more than I ever had.

I'D JUST FINISHED A MEETING WITH A FEW OF TITAN'S regional managers. Now I had a short break before I met with Kyle Livingston and Vincent Hunt after lunch. We were putting all of her products on international shelves. Kyle Livingston was only along for the ride because he chose to work with Titan over Vincent. He'd remained loyal to her, so she wanted to do the same for him once Vincent had a new offer on the table.

It worked out well for Kyle.

I sat at Titan's white desk and looked over the folder Jessica had left next to my laptop. My tablet kept lighting up with emails that I needed to address for my own businesses. I hadn't abandoned all of my work to take care of hers. Instead, I was handling two things at once. It made for exceptionally long days. After hitting the gym, managing two empires, and taking a few breaks in between, by the time I got home, I was ready to go to sleep so I could wake up and do it all over again.

Jessica spoke through the intercom. "There's a woman here asking for Titan. I told her she wasn't available, but she could meet with you."

I held the button down with my forefinger. "What does she want?"

"She wouldn't share that with me."

After Titan had been shot, I'd become a paranoid man. Even the sanest people weren't what they seemed. If you crossed someone in the wrong way, there was no predicting what would happen next. The information Jessica was giving me was mysterious—and a bit concerning. "What's her name?"

"Bridget Creed."

That didn't ring any bells.

"She seems a bit distressed."

"In what way?" I asked.

"When she asked about Titan, she seemed upset."

Maybe this was someone Titan knew. She could be a colleague or an acquaintance or something. "Send her in."

"Alright."

A moment later, Jessica opened the door and allowed the woman to step inside.

She was in her fifties, but she held herself like a young woman. In a black dress with heels, she had a slim figure. She had brown hair that stopped just past her shoulders. A gold necklace hung from her throat, and she wore a wedding ring on her left hand.

I understood what Jessica meant when she said this woman was distressed.

I could see the sadness around her eyes, the stress in her tight mouth. If she weren't frowning so severely, she would actually be a pretty woman.

She walked up to my desk and didn't shake my hand. "Thank you for seeing me, Thorn."

I didn't appreciate the way she addressed me so casually, not when I'd never met her until that moment. "It's Mr. Cutler." I slowly rose to my feet and extended my hand.

"I apologize," she said quickly, sighing under her breath. "I feel like I know you..."

"Why?"

"I just...I see you on the news all the time."

For bullshit that wasn't even true. I returned to my seat and kept up my cold stare, unsure what I was dealing with. She didn't seem dangerous, just a little uneasy. I sat back as I examined her, my guard up.

She didn't take a seat. "When will Titan be back in?"

"She's still recovering at home. She'll be back to work eventually, but she needs more time."

In the time since she stepped into the office, she'd barely blinked two times. Her gaze was glued to my face like she was afraid to miss a single instant.

"It's been taking her a while...were there other complications? Will she be alright?"

Everyone asked me how Titan was doing. Some people genuinely cared, and others didn't. But even the people who actually knew her didn't look as upset as this woman. Once it'd been declared that Titan had survived the surgery and was making a recovery, everyone calmed down and started talking about someone else. But this woman's chest was rising and falling with rapid breathing like she couldn't get enough air. She was as panicked as I'd been sitting in the waiting room. "Titan is the strongest person I know. If anyone can make a complete recovery, it's her. I wouldn't worry too much about it."

That didn't erase the lines of worry on her face. If she had nothing left to say, she should thank me for my time and leave. But she stayed put like there was something else to discuss.

"How do you know her?" If they were close, she would call Titan directly. But since she was standing in front of me instead of Titan, that told me their friendship was more an acquaintance.

It was the first time she broke eye contact. She looked at the white desk, examining the vase of lilies and the gray MacBook. Her eyes combed over the desk, searching for something, before she turned back to me. "I was out of the country for the last few weeks. When I got back to town the other day, I heard the news. I didn't know what else to do, so I came here..."

Why didn't she answer my question?

"I just need to know that she's going to be alright..."

"I'm sure she will be."

She gave a slight nod, her chest still rising and falling rapidly. She took a slight step back from the desk, drawing away from me.

I rose to my feet again. "Should I tell her you stopped by?"

"Uh...no." She tucked her brown hair behind her ear then turned away from my desk. "Thank you for your time, Mr. Cutler."

Something in my gut said something was wrong here. Titan would never be acquainted with someone who lacked professional grace. This woman seemed off-balance, far too affected by Titan's tragedy than an objective person should be. "Ms. Creed?"

She turned around when she reached the door, just as much sadness in her eyes as there was when she walked in.

"How do you know her?"

Her hand moved to the handle, and she rested it there for a moment. It seemed like she was going to give me an answer judging by the way she opened her lips slightly. But something must have changed her mind, because she yanked the handle down and walked off at a quick pace, like I might decide to chase her.

Whatever her relationship was with Titan, she didn't want me to know about it.

It made me wonder if Titan even knew about it.

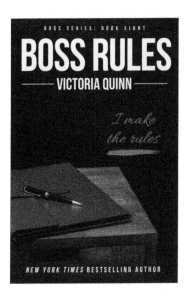

Printed in Great Britain
by Amazon